THORNS AND FORGIVENESS

TWISTED LEGACY DUET

CORALEE JUNE

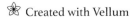

For that asshole professor at Texas State University that told me I'd never have a career in writing. I forgot your name, but one day the world will know mine.

PROLOGUE

Vera

Ten years ago

I loved watching Mom apply her makeup in our tiny apartment bathroom. It was like watching someone spray paint the side of a brick building. She had all these fancy brushes and covered every inch of her face. I sat on the toilet, my legs swinging back and forth as I told her about Ronnie McIntyre pushing me on the playground. She smacked her ruby lips lined thickly, and stared at her reflection.

The way Mom celebrated her face felt revolutionary to me. She was always fussing about the advantages of pretty people.

"You tell Ronnie to eat shit the next time he pushes you, Vera," she said while rolling another layer of mascara onto her clumpy eyelashes. "We don't let boys push us around or hurt us. Garner women are strong, baby." She finished putting on her mask and then frowned at her reflection for a moment too long. "We are fucking strong," she whispered.

"Okay, Mom," I promised, because that was the sensible thing for an eight-year-old to say. She continued applying her dollar store war paint.

"So strong..." she repeated, this time her voice bouncing off the linoleum floor with a vengeance.

1

My sluggish brain felt swollen and heavy. Every fucking pore in my throbbing body reeked of alcohol and regret. The pounding at the base of my skull assured me that I still had a pulse, despite trying to drown my pathetic heart with whiskey last night.

I wanted to cut off my circulation and numb my body from the ground up to escape the burning, throbbing, *aching* pain.

The older I got, the more getting blackout drunk lost its appeal. It was one thing to use alcohol like a weapon to get back at my father. I loved to indulge in destruction, then fuck some random girl on the living room floor. But this time, the only person getting stabbed with a broken whiskey glass was me. Metaphorically speaking, of course. Fuck. It felt like I had glass splinters in my brain.

My mouth was dry, as if I'd spent the last twelve hours chewing on cotton balls. My stomach churned. Shame like razor blades cut through me the moment I opened my eyes and saw my best friend's face.

"Rise and shine, asshole." Jess thrusted a platter of greasy bacon in my face, and I slowly sat up. The smell was too much. I was on my couch, buck ass naked and covered in a sheen of sweat. I needed to puke, shower, then eat.

"Good morning," I replied, my deep voice like sandpaper on my vocal cords. "Has Vera called?"

Even though I felt half dead, she was the first thing on my mind. She was the *only* thing consuming my thoughts these days. I wasn't used to thinking of anything but ruining my brother. The obsessive estrangement took a back seat the moment

I met Vera Garner. But like a disease, my hate for Joseph bled through the one good thing in my life and ate at it, the cancerous loathing too powerful and potent to ignore.

And yeah, maybe I was being melodramatic. There was plenty of pussy out there. But Vera was different. This was different. Our whole goddamn story was more haunting than my nightmares, than finding my mother's dying body in the upstairs bathroom, or having my arm snapped by my deranged brother. It was the kind of heartbreak that stuck with you.

When Jess didn't answer me, I asked again. "Well? Did she call?" I wasn't sure what answer I wanted to spill from my best friend's lips.

Jess rolled her eyes and shook her head in annoyance. "Oh! You mean the girl I *told* you to be honest with when shit started to get serious between the two of you?" I wasn't in the mood for my best friend's *I told you so* lecture, but my head hurt too damn much to argue with her. Jess continued. "I thought you forgot about her. You know, since you were trying to bring home a blond divorcée with a hard-on for your last name at the bar yesterday."

I pinched the bridge of my nose and winced.

Shit. "I didn't...did I?" It was fucking trash that I couldn't even remember.

"No. She leaned in for a kiss, and you started crying like a little bitch about Vera. Her metaphorical dick went soft after that." Jess let out a huff before setting the platter piled with bacon on the coffee table. "You know I don't judge. If you want to fuck your way through town and drink yourself to death, go for it. I love you unconditionally, bro, but even *I* think it's shitty. I thought we were going out for a couple drinks so you could get your head on straight and figure out how to get Vera back. I didn't realize you'd go on a full fucking bender. And put some clothes on, I'm tired of your elephant dick staring at me."

My *elephant dick* was missing Vera something fierce. Despite being hung over as hell, my traitorous hard-on was ready to track my girl down and remind her how fucking good our bodies fit together. I was addicted to her. The feel of her soft skin. Her little moans. When she came, it was one of the few times she finally let go. She squeezed my cock like...*fuck*. I can't even explain it. Spectacular. It was fucking spectacular. There wasn't a good enough metaphor to describe the feeling. If I were a boring, basic-ass man, I'd say it felt like heaven. But even feeling like shit, I was neither boring nor basic. I sure as hell wasn't going to compare perfection to some mythical place I'd never been to before. It should be sinful. Devilish. Dangerous. If I had one last breath in the world, I'd inhale deeply and use the remaining oxygen in my lungs to scream that Vera was mine and mine alone—*choke*—she was mine, mine, mine, mine, mine—*exhale*—and that word would play on repeat until my eyes rolled back and my lips turned blue. One long, run-on declaration of suffocation.

Crazy. I was going fucking crazy. Did I do drugs last night? It was like I popped a little white pill called melancholy.

"Whatever," I answered before standing up. The fucking room tilted to the side. More bile traveled up my throat, and the throbbing slammed hard between my eyes. I nearly toppled over. Waves of vertigo hit me like a punch to the balls. After a few minutes of overwhelming nausea and dizziness, Jess sent a pair of underwear flying through the air, hitting me in the face. "Thanks," I croaked before slowly putting it on, somehow managing not to fall on my face.

"Go take a shower so you don't smell like the men's bathroom at a bar. I've got an emergency stash of chocolate, and I don't have to work today. We can stop by the flower shop and get Vera some roses. Bitches love roses. You'll apologize and give her a smolder so we can all go back to normal." Jess was pacing the floors in front of me, a determined scowl on her pretty face.

I ran a hand through my greasy hair. I thought about my perfect Petal and what roses represented in her life. Maybe her mom was right. I ruined her. "I'm not getting her roses," I replied softly before stomping toward my bathroom. "And I'm not going to apologize."

I wanted Vera Garner more than anything in the world. I didn't just want her body, I craved every inch of her soul. Being away from her was already making me a miserable fucker. But I wasn't going to be selfish about this.

Jess cursed and followed after me. "And why the fuck not?"

I grabbed my toothbrush and stared at my reflection. The dark circles under my eyes made it look like I got punched in the face. My lips were cracked. My skin pale. Jess leaned against the doorjamb, waiting for my answer. "I'm not going to be another person in Vera's life that demands her forgiveness."

I turned on the faucet and started brushing my

teeth. Jess gave me an incredulous look, her brown eyes wide as she gaped at me. "What the hell is that supposed to mean?"

Vera's mother hurt her over and over and over again. And every single time, Vera forgave her. It was a toxic, never-ending cycle that I wanted nothing to do with. Even if we somehow moved past this, I knew I would just hurt her again. I was too fucked up to make this work. Eventually, I'd become just like Lilah, abusing the privilege of Vera's gentle, unconditional love for the sake of my own ego and selfish needs.

I spit my toothpaste out and wiped my mouth. "Just drop it, okay?"

Jess shook her head. "Oh no, you don't. If you won't go to her, then I'll just bring her here."

"I wouldn't bother. I'll just send her away. And I won't be nice about it either."

Jess was always picking at my scabs, refusing to let me just sit with a decision. Most of the time, I appreciated her tenacity. Jess was brave, hard-hitting, and determined. She didn't let me wallow in self-pity, and she sure as hell didn't let me go on nuclear self-destructive benders. But right now, I didn't want her invasive opinions. I'd made up my mind, and I was going to stick to it—for Vera's sake.

She pressed on, blocking the bathroom exit with her body when I moved to leave. "Martyr shit. This is some fucked up martyr shit, Hamilton. You like Vera. So what if you lied? Apologize, do better, and move on with your motherfucking life. She's Sycamore Tree, Hamilton. Not to mention, Vera might be the only girl I've ever liked for you. Win her back. Easy."

I let out a huff. Jess made it seem so simple. Sure, I could probably *win Vera back*. My girl was sympathetic, empathetic, compassionate, and loving. Her heart was an endless well the rest of the world liked to drink from. If I wanted her back in my bed by tonight, I probably could have her. I didn't mean that to sound cocky or assuming. She was a forgiving soul, and it was one of the things that immediately drew me in about her. But it was the *moving on with my life* part that made me stop dead in my tracks. How long until I was fucking up again? How long until I ruined shit and had to ask for her forgiveness?

Being arrogant was a lonely battle.

"I didn't like her that much," I lied with bitter, false acceptance, the taste of it like gunpowder on my tongue. The truth was, I liked her *too much*. Hell, I loved Vera Garner and wanted to spend all day wrapped up in her mind. She was too good for me—

and too damn good for this fucked up family. I used her as a pawn, and there was no coming back from that. Even if Vera was willing to forgive me, I struggled with forgiving myself.

Jess was pissed, her words booming at me. "That's some bullshit. I've never seen you like this. I know you care about Vera. Pull your head out of your ass and go get your girl, Hamilton!" Jess stomped her combat boots on the linoleum floor. Her tantrum made me want to smile. My best friend was loyal to a fault, and if she had to choose, she would always choose me. But Jess liked Vera. She didn't just want things to work out for my sake.

"So I can just hurt her again? You didn't see her fucking face, Jess. She risked it all for me, and I took advantage of that. Vera was devastated. She got this defeated look in her eyes. Like, the flickering light went completely out. A struck match in a motherfucking hurricane. It stuck with me. I've only seen her like that one other time: when her mother showed up, bloodied and blue on my doorstep. I'm not going to be another person in her life that makes her feel like shit. I'm not going to ruin the girl I love."

Jess's expression softened. She reached out and awkwardly wrapped me in a hug. I let her, mostly because I needed it. "Hamilton. You aren't going to ruin her." Jess squeezed me one more time before pulling away and looking up at me. "You made a mistake. The difference between you and her monster of a mother is that you feel remorse. I mean, fuck, bro, you look like shit. And you're torn up about this. I know you. I know you better than anyone in this fucking world." She chewed on her lip ring for a moment, then shrugged. "I think Vera needs you. I think you challenge her. I don't trust Joseph. And if I were you, I'd put aside the martyr bullshit to protect your girl. If you accept defeat, you're just delivering her and Lilah to Joseph with a bow."

I clenched my jaw and looked at the ground. Jess was right. I couldn't just walk away. I had to figure out a way to protect Vera from the disaster that was my family while keeping my distance. "Are you going to keep blocking me in?" I asked. Jess was a pain in the ass when she wanted to be. It was one of the many reasons why I loved her so goddamn much.

"Are you going to keep pretending like you don't love that girl?" Jess asked before crossing her arms over her chest. I frowned at her.

"Fuck you, Jess," I said before dropping my boxers and spinning around to get in the shower.

"You can't run from this!" my best friend sang on an exhale as I turned on the shower and got inside. Hot water poured over my skin, warming me from the inside out. Though the water felt good, my pulsing veins still ached. I needed coffee. And pain killers. "Stop ignoring me, Hamilton."

After quickly washing my hair, I grabbed my shower gel and ran it over my abs just as Jess yanked open the shower curtain and glared at me. "If you wanted a show, you just had to ask," I replied in such a sleazy way that I internally cringed at my words.

"Shut the fuck up and call me after you've shaved your asscrack, motherfucker," Jess answered before pressing her lips into a fine line and staring at me. I waited. And waited. We had a silent, naked standoff.

It was me who eventually caved.

"What? Can we please just move on? I'm done having this conversation," I growled before rinsing off.

"I just think you're making a huge mistake—an even bigger mistake than using her to get back at your brother. Hell, I thought this whole Saint thing was fucked up from the beginning." That pissed me off. I shut off the water and grabbed a nearby towel. "You weren't saying that when you suggested we stage everything at Infinity's show so her band could get some free PR," I snapped back before drying off.

"Yeah, well, that was before I got to know Vera. I thought we were screwing over the Beauregards, not ruining some innocent chick's life. You should have been honest with her before it snowballed this far."

I slammed my palm on the wall and yelled. "You think I don't know that? You think I don't know that I used her in the worst possible way and that I didn't just lie once, but I lied every fucking time we were together—every time we fucked—every time I got closer and closer? Figure out what you want, Jess, because one second, you're telling me to show up at her doorstep with some flowers and a goddamn smolder so I can collect her forgiveness like it's Halloween candy, and then the next minute you're telling me that I'm complete shit for lying to her. You're proving my point."

"And what is your point exactly?" Jess asked.

"I don't want Vera's forgiveness. I hurt her, Jess. I fucking hurt her. I don't deserve Vera," I said, my tone defeated.

Jess finally let me pass, and I marched over to my bedroom, where my sheets were still messed up from the last time Vera spent the night. Where the smell of her clung to every inch of the space. Where her clothes lay crumbled in a pile on the floor. Where her handwritten notes for class sat on my dresser.

We'd only known each other for a little while, but she'd already taken over my life. I was always so guarded, never letting people come to my house, pushing them away before I could even slide off my condom. I usually fled and forgot people.

But not Vera. I wanted her under my skin. I needed her in my life completely, staining my existence. I grabbed a pair of black sweats and put them on before finding a shirt. "I just want you to be happy, Hamilton." Jess sniffled. Yeah, I wanted that too. "You know what Joseph is capable of. I really want you to consider that maybe you could protect Vera. Maybe you'd be really, really good for her."

Fuck yeah, I knew what Joseph was capable of. Jess knew about my broken arm.

And the broken nose.

The chipped tooth.

The kick to the balls.

The pillow over my face.

The bleach on my skin.

The burn marks on my thigh.

Joseph needed an outlet for his insanity, and I

was his own personal punching bag. My mother couldn't protect me, and my father didn't care.

I chewed on my battle scars. Broken homes started wars if you weren't careful.

Jess continued, "And I don't want this to make you spiral. I've seen how you cope, and I don't know how you're going to react to a full-blown broken heart."

I fought the urge to scowl. I knew Jess was coming from a good place, but how I coped wasn't as big of a deal as she made it out to be. I was fine. On the anniversary of my mother's death, I didn't want to think about my family's shitty past. But with Vera? I wanted to feel every ounce of this pain. I wanted to sit and absorb what I'd done. Last night, I'd gotten drunk, but it didn't numb me. I just wanted to...sit. I wanted to settle in and not leave my fucking house.

"Want to go to the gym? Or maybe we could..."

"I don't want to do anything, Jess. Actually, I kind of just want to be alone for a little while."

Jess reared back and placed her hand on her chest as if I'd slapped her. I might as well have. We did everything together. When shit went down, she was my rock. But not right now. I just wanted time to myself.

"Oh," Jess said in a dejected tone. "Okay. Are you

sure? We can veg out and order from your favorite Greek restaurant—"

"I just want to be alone," I repeated.

"You're not going to do anything stupid, are you?" Jess asked, unconvinced.

"I'm not going to leave my fucking house. Just go. Please. Thanks for taking care of me last night. I just need time."

Jess let out a shaky exhale. "Okay. But like if you go anywhere—"

"I won't."

"If you want to do anything—"

"I don't."

Jess nodded. "Oh. I took Little Mama on a walk earlier, but she'll probably need to go outside again soon... Want me to stay until then?"

At hearing her name, my dog got up from her bed in the corner of the room and padded over to me. "I've got it," I replied before patting Little Mama on the head and settling in on the couch.

Jess silently stood there for a moment before sighing in defeat and excusing herself.

My father taught me that we were all born with hearts made of glass. Delicate, murderous little tools pounding in our chests. I just needed to take some time and toughen it up with a bit of fire and agony.

After all, I was a Beauregard. And Beauregards didn't suffer from empathy, remorse, and guilt. We stepped barefoot on the shattered shards like little psychopaths, proving to the world that we didn't need pretty emotions to survive.

2

VERA

*M*y mom's designer luggage was weighed down with clothes, regret, and empty promises. I struggled to carry each bag by myself, but I managed.

I brought the heavy suitcases into Jack Beauregard's home as my mother stood on the porch. Her black cardigan was wrapped tightly around her body, and she had her chin raised in indignation, looking down on the property like a scorned queen. Mom's sunken-in cheeks hollowed as she chewed on her thoughts. Though she was silent, her body language screamed at me.

I knew she was mad. I'd broken the cardinal rule: I interfered in her happily ever after.

"Jack should be home later. I have a roast in the crock pot. I thought maybe tonight we could bake cookies," I offered on a grunt before dropping one of her particularly heavy suitcases. She stared at the tree line in the distance, not bothering to respond. "We used to bake cookies all the time. Remember, Mom?"

Nothing. No answer. The silence stretched like barbed wire between two fence posts. Pulled tight, sharp with guarded intent.

Mom wasn't happy about being away from her husband and back in Connecticut. And from what I gathered, Joseph wasn't happy about Jack's meddling either. I didn't get to listen in on the negotiations, but it took some finesse to get my mother on a plane. Why my mother didn't jump at the chance to get the hell away from her husband was a mystery to me. I saw the painful bruises. I knew what my stepfather was capable of. But perhaps she sensed the same uncertainties about Jack as I did. I wasn't sure if I could trust him, but I didn't really have any other options.

My grandfather claimed that he was done covering up his oldest son's sins, but I didn't feel comfortable trusting his sudden change of heart. And until this morning, I wasn't even sure he was capable of keeping up his end of the deal. It had been four days since I agreed to his little arrangement. Four days since I found out my relationship with Hamilton was nothing but a lie. Four days of embarrassment and regret. Four days to get lost in my thoughts and come up with a game plan for saving my mom and abiding by Jack's terms.

He wanted me to mend his relationship with Hamilton, but I wanted nothing to do with the man who broke my heart, then disappeared. Hamilton had completely ghosted me. No calls, texts, or emails. I should have been pleased by that, but the selfish part of me had hoped that he would at least try to reach out and apologize. My ego wanted him to grovel. But in the last four days, I'd gotten nothing but radio silence.

I really did mean nothing to Hamilton Beauregard.

Even though it broke my heart to think that he never cared, I knew that this would make my job much easier. Jack's plan hinged on the idea that Hamilton loved me enough to mend their relationship. Little did my grandfather know his son didn't even like me enough to send a text.

Maybe Hamilton took my words in the woods to heart. In the midst of my pain, I begged him to never speak to me again. But I suppose a part of me pushed him away to see how hard he would push to get back to me. It was wrong and immature, but I've always been the person fighting for the relationships in my life. Just once, I wanted someone to fight for me.

At least my mother was here, safe and sound.

When I picked her up at the airport earlier this afternoon, I had to force myself not to sob at the sight of her. While clenching my teeth, I ran my eyes up and down my battered and beaten mother. Her make-up was caked on, likely hiding the bruises littering her swollen face. She looked half starved to death and downright miserable. The first words she said to me were, "I hate it here." I didn't understand what was so bad about being back in Connecticut. I was here, wasn't I? That had to count for something.

Even now, she looked almost sick. "Don't bother unpacking my things, Vera. I'm not staying for long," she finally murmured after I lugged the last Louis

Vuitton suitcase into the house. She tore her eyes away from the yard where just a while ago she celebrated her marriage. With a huff, she followed me inside.

"Unpacking won't hurt anything. Besides, Jack said you're going to stay here while Joseph acclimates to his new job and until your new house is built. That could take months." I prayed that it took months—years—eternity.

"We were doing just fine until Jack called. My husband was very angry, Vera. Very, very angry. I can't believe you told Jack about...about..." She cleared her throat before continuing, "Um, my last visit. You're still young. You don't understand, Vera."

She's lucky I didn't tell the police about her last visit. She might want to shove her husband's abuse under the rug, but I refused to. Mom showed up half dead, and I was supposed to just let it go? No. I refused. Letting out a sigh, I continued, "There isn't much to understand. Joseph hurt you. I didn't know what to do—"

"Well, you shouldn't have called Jack. Joseph didn't *mean* to hurt me. Sometimes his anger gets the best of him. He just has a lot of expectations of me, and I have to try harder to meet them. I was so close. I've been working out. I've made his favorite dinners.

I pick up his dry cleaning. I wear his favorite colors and ignore the nights he works late. I'm his fucking wife. I can do this. I can be what he needs. I just needed more time. You don't get it." Mom's words meshed together like a rambling broken record. What had Joseph done to her?

She was right about one thing, though. I didn't understand, and I wasn't sure that any explanation my mother gave me would help me to make sense of it all.

I let out a sigh and moved her belongings to the first-floor bedroom Jack had set up for her, giving my mother more time to obsess about what coming here would mean for her marriage, and when I walked back, I caught the tail end of her mumbling to herself. "He's going to find someone else..."

"You're his wife! You're married, Mom. You already got him. You aren't responsible for his actions. You aren't responsible for his lack of integrity. If he chooses to cheat, that's his fault. Not yours," I said, my voice stern and harsh.

Her lip curled, and she spun to face me. "You don't know anything. You don't understand what it means to keep a man like Joseph's attention—to keep him happy and agreeable. We were already hanging by a thread."

Good, I wanted to say. Let the thread snap. Shatter. Dissolve and disappear. Let us both live our lives in peace. I wanted to destroy anything that tethered us to the Beauregards.

How could she possibly settle for a relationship like that?

"If I married a man like Joseph, a man who beat me up and cheated on me, would you be happy for me?" I bravely asked. I just wanted her to see things through my eyes. Nothing seemed worth her well-being and happiness.

Mom scowled. "At the rate you're going, you'd be lucky to pull someone like Joseph. I had everything set up for you. Sent you to a school filled with eligible men that have trust funds and financial security people like us can only dream of. But you threw it away."

Her words hurt, but I pressed on, desperate to get through to her. "But what if I didn't? What if I married a man like Joseph? A man who hurt me without a care."

She inhaled deeply and turned to look at me. "I think we established with Hamilton that it doesn't matter if I approve of the men you date. You've always been so reckless. I had such high hopes for you, Vera. I wanted you to do things right. Wait until marriage and find yourself a wealthy man that can take care of you. Not settle for a man like Hamilton." Her snarky tone sent a wave of anger through me.

I thought about the rose she once compared me to and wondered if there were any petals left. If I was a pretty flower, then Hamilton crushed me in his fist. Hamilton was a mistake, one that left wounds you couldn't see, but were still just as painful.

Hamilton was still a gut-wrenching topic. The man was only with me to sell me out. So much pain could have been avoided had I just listened to my mother and kept my distance. And the worst part was, I couldn't even validate my fragile mother with the truth. Jack wanted me to mend his family— continue on like nothing had happened. He expected me to bridge the gap between Hamilton and me, overcoming his absence with determination and pity.

I changed the subject to avoid telling her what had happened. A year ago, it would have felt unnatural not to tell her. There was a time I thought we shared everything. Now, it was just another secret, another lie piled like bricks between us. I had to approach her like a sleeping lion, delicately tiptoeing across her cavernous heart like anything could startle it. "You're staying with Jack. You like Jack. I doubt Joseph will forget his wife."

"He just wants to hide me away. He's embarrassed by me. Ashamed of me."

"Mom. This is only temporary." *At least until whatever toxic spell he has you under has worn off.*

"Just like my marriage," she spat. "I'll have nothing. I'll have to work as a...maid and a waitress. I'll be a nobody again. A joke. How am I supposed to go back now that I've had a taste of *everything*?"

Everything was just another word for empty. She could fill her life up with designer luxuries and money and influence, but it meant absolutely nothing. Joseph was still an abuser. The Beauregards were still twisted liars.

"Mom. I'm here for you, okay? Everything is going to be okay."

She looked at me, her eyes dragging up and down my body with such scrutiny that I wanted to scream until every damn window in this massive house burst. I wondered if she noticed the bags under my eyes, or the oversized clothes on my body. Did she see how broken I looked? How destroyed Hamilton left me? Or was she so wrapped up in her own problems, that she couldn't see past the tip of her own nose? "You need to eat," she murmured. So maybe she had noticed.

"So do you," I said.

"Are you doing well in school?" she pressed.

I was getting straight A's but had no friends. No life outside of class.

"I've got great grades."

"That's good, Vera. I'm going to my room for the night. Tell Jack thank you for letting me stay here and that I'll properly greet him tomorrow." She straightened her spine, shutting off her emotions in the blink of an eye.

I wanted to pressure her to join us for dinner, mostly because I wasn't willing to eat with Jack alone. I knew he was going to ask me about Hamilton.

"Goodnight," Mom said before I could argue. Realizing it was hopeless to have a reasonable conversation with her, I left her to sulk so I could go check on dinner. Jack would be arriving any minute now, and I wanted to have the table set before he arrived.

I didn't trust Jack. I didn't like that he was holding me hostage with an agreement that would protect my mother and safeguard my college tuition.

The front door opened, and I listened attentively

as footsteps clicked across the tiled floors toward me. "Hello, Vera," he said Jack wore a sharkskin three-piece suit, and his hair was slicked back. The dark brown briefcase in his grasp drew my eye.

"Hello, Jack. How was work?" I greeted politely.

"Work has been...difficult lately. I spent an entire day with my team of accountants. I will never understand why someone would want a career crunching numbers." He let out a sigh.

"Sounds like a long day," I replied conversationally. "Dinner is ready."

"Will your mother be joining us?"

"She's tired from the flight," I answered simply, the thinly veiled lie flowing off my tongue.

Jack looked lost in thought for a moment as I grabbed two dinner plates. "My late wife was tired often." I didn't like that he was comparing my mother to his deceased wife, but I nodded. "I'd like to speak with her soon. I have a few questions about Joseph." Jack set down his briefcase and breathed in the smell of dinner. I watched him, my entire body on edge. Jack continued speaking as I served both of us. "I'm sorry it took me a bit longer to get her here than we originally agreed upon. Joseph wasn't as willing to let her out of his sight. I'm not sure if it's because he genuinely likes having her around or if he fears losing control over her by sending her away. My son has always been a selfish fucker."

I breathed in. "How *did* you get Mom here, by the way?"

Jack answered easily. "I told him that some photos of Lilah with a black eye had surfaced and that he perhaps needed some space to acclimate to DC and cool down. I also told him I wouldn't stop the photos from making the papers if he didn't comply."

"You blackmailed him? Do you even have photos?"

Jack grinned. "I was bluffing, but he doesn't have to know that. My son doesn't like airing out his dirty laundry. It is easy to bury your own faults deep when you only have to convince yourself that you're perfect. It gets harder to do that when the world is pointing its finger at you. I'm ashamed of what he's done, Vera. I'm not sure he would have let your mother come here if I hadn't done that."

It was jarring to hear Jack speak so candidly about his son. "Well, let's eat, yes?"

"Yes. Speaking of, there's plenty of food here. Why don't you invite Hamilton to dinner?"

I prayed the floor would swallow me up. My chest constricted with a palpable pain that made breathing difficult. I knew this was coming, but I still hated it all the same. "You want me to invite Hamilton to dinner?" I asked.

"Yes," Jack replied simply. "I would."

"He won't come."

"I think he will. It's worth a try."

I let out a shaky breath and stared Jack down. A deal was a deal, I'd just hoped for more time to convince my heart that Hamilton was bad news.

"Fine. I doubt he'll even answer," I said.

"I think my son will surprise you," Jack replied easily. His cocky behavior reminded me that he'd built a political career with that smug smile. Pulling my cell phone from my pocket, I clicked Hamilton's name and turned on the speaker. I wanted Jack to listen to this. It made the call feel less personal.

It rang.

And rang.

And rang.

Then went to voicemail. I breathed a sigh of relief and looked up at Jack.

"Leave a message," he said.

I ground my teeth as the line beeped.

"Hey, Hamilton. Um. I just was calling to see if you wanted to talk?" My voice sounded lame. "I made dinner if you're hungry. Feel free to call me. Or don't." I quickly added that last part, then winced. "Okay. Bye. Hope you're doing well."

I hung up the phone and let out a huff of air. "See? He didn't answer."

"He could be busy. Let's eat before dinner gets cold, hmm?"

My heart was still pounding from the embarrassment and adrenaline of my call to Hamilton. I felt like a fool, leaving him that message. At best, Hamilton would think I was pathetic and block my number. He wasn't the type of man to like clingy women.

I'd just sat down at the table with my food when my phone started ringing.

My eyes connected with Jack's. He grinned triumphantly, and the eager look on his face made me rage. Sure enough, Hamilton had called me back.

I answered after taking a deep breath, making sure to put him on speaker so Jack could hear the conversation. It made it feel less...personal. "Hello?" I croaked. I'd never felt so small or so stupid.

"Why the fuck did you call me?" Hamilton asked. His booming voice made me tremble. It was an extremely unexpected greeting.

"I just..."

"You just what? Thought we could talk about our feelings?"

I squeezed my eyes to force the tears from falling. Why did he sound so angry? I was the one that got hurt. "I just wanted to—"

"You just want my dick, baby? Is that it?"

"I just wanted to talk," I repeated. "I thought maybe—"

"You thought maybe you meant something to me? You thought maybe I *wanted* to talk to you? Sorry, but if you wanted to hear me apologize so we could fuck and make up, then you're wasting your time."

I looked at Jack, who was scowling. Good. This needed to happen. Even if it broke me. Even if Hamilton took what little hope I had left and stomped on it. "I was mistaken. I apologize."

"Fuck yeah, you're mistaken. Don't call me again. I don't want your forgiveness. I don't need your used-up pussy, either."

"I'm sorry," I croaked.

"Say it out loud, Vera. Say *Hamilton doesn't want my used-up pussy.* It'll help it sink. In. Go on."

"I'm not saying that," I whispered, ferocious anguish boiling to the surface.

"Aw, you almost sound convincing. You do

whatever I ask, don't you, Vera? You're so easy to manipulate."

"Hamilton!" Jack interrupted. "Stop that right now. The poor girl just wanted to chat."

My cheeks were stained with tears. My heart pounded with a pain so achingly haunting that I had to catch my breath. I knew that Jack speaking would send Hamilton further into a rage that there was no coming back from. A few beats of time passed. "What are you doing with my father?" Hamilton asked, his voice terrifyingly calm.

"My mother is staying at Jack's house for a little while. I'm here helping her get settled." Hamilton went silent. "I'm sorry for calling, Hamilton. I won't do it again."

"Let me be very clear, baby," Hamilton said in a sinister tone. "I don't like you. I barely even *wanted* you. I used you up, little rose. Now there's nothing left but the stem, and I've got no use for thorns. But hey," he added as I nearly crumbled from the pain, "thanks for the pussy. It was fun while it lasted."

"You're disgusting," I barked, the outburst surprising me. "Let me make myself clear then, Hamilton. You hurt me. You should be groveling right now, begging for my forgiveness. You're lucky I even called, you bastard!"

"Then why did you call, hmm?"

My throat closed up. "I—I don't..."

"Exactly. I'm not begging for something I don't want, Petal," he whispered. The endearing nickname caught me by surprise.

"Goodbye," I replied, then hung up the phone before he could hurt me anymore. My hands trembled from the confrontation. This was why I'd been putting it off. I didn't want further proof that Hamilton didn't give two shits about me. "Happy?" I asked Jack on a broken sob. I'd never felt so used in my life.

Jack, seemingly undeterred, grabbed his plate and waltzed over to the kitchen table. "He's just hurting. He'll come around."

"Did you not hear him?" I asked with a scoff. "He's not going to come around. He wants nothing to do with me, Jack."

Jack sat down and started picking at his food. "He's just lashing out. He didn't mean it. Be a good girl and wipe your eyes. Painful words aren't meant to hurt if they're lies." I ignored my plate with my mouth gaped open incredulously. Jack wanted me to keep trying? After that? "Oh, don't look at me like that. Sticks and stones, Vera. The boy loves you."

"The Beauregards don't do love," I snapped.

"I know my son."

"You don't know him at all," I argued.

"I know that we have a deal, and you're going to try your best, or I'll make things very difficult for your mother and you. I promised to take care of everything if you help me with Hamilton. We both have jobs to do, and you can't do yours if you're sobbing at my table. Maybe you need a makeover..."

I shook my head and closed my eyes, more tears streaming down my cheeks. I couldn't believe this. I knew trusting Jack was a bad decision. "You'll make me do this? Even though Hamilton has made it clear that he hates me?" I asked.

"He doesn't hate you. Toughen up a bit. And eat your dinner, it's getting cold."

I couldn't imagine how I could eat. My stomach was twisted in knots. How could Hamilton treat me so poorly when it was me who was hurt? It was me who was betrayed. The whole situation with Saint was still a bitter pill to swallow, and now I had his brutal words to pile on top of it.

I was still processing the Saint dynamic. There was something that had been bugging me about it, and I knew Jack would be able to explain it to me. I cleared my throat, forcing my emotions to settle so I could get some answers. "Can I ask you something?"

"You can ask whatever you'd like."

"Did you know that Saint is Hamilton's brother?"

"No. I didn't," he answered instantly. "I knew Hamilton had a half brother somewhere out there, but I didn't realize the paparazzi hounding us was him." Jack took a slow bite, chewing his food meticulously before continuing in a calm voice, unaffected by any of this. "Saint's mother isn't a bad person. Her name is Gabby. She interned at my campaign office. We had a quick affair during a moment of weakness. A couple years after Hamilton was born, she married well, had a son, and moved on with her life. She didn't think about Hamilton. She didn't care. I didn't bother to keep tabs on her because it didn't matter. She didn't matter. She wanted to keep everything a secret. Gabby had aspirations to pioneer across the political landscape. She didn't want her bastard son with a politician to be public information, because it affected her credibility. Her husband didn't even know. When Joseph went to the press with that story, it ruined her career before it truly started."

"Such a fucking double standard," I gritted.

"I agree. Women have to work twice as hard to be taken seriously. They labeled her as some wide-eyed coed so willing to do anything to get ahead, who abandoned her child. I won't pretend to know Saint's story, but I'm assuming that his vendetta stemmed from watching his mother's career go down the toilet. I heard a rumor that she ended up getting a divorce. In the beginning, I tried to help, but she wanted nothing to do with me. Hell, I haven't seen her in years. We ruined her life, Hamilton and I."

"Hamilton didn't ask to be born. And it was Joseph that leaked the story," I argued. Perhaps I was sensitive about blaming unwanted children for existing, but I didn't like how Jack worded that.

"You're correct, Vera."

I looked down at my feet. "Are you a bad guy, Jack?" I tentatively asked, already knowing the answer, but needing to hear it out loud so I could know for sure.

"Yes," he replied simply.

Suddenly losing my appetite, I walked out of the kitchen, out the door, and away from the family that broke me.

I'm pretty sure I no longer had a job.

I was supposed to be on a flight headed to the rig this morning, but instead, I'd gotten on my motorcycle and headed toward Jack's house.

Considering my father's net worth was 13.7 billion dollars and I would inherit half of it upon his death, it felt ridiculous to mourn the loss of seventy thousand a year doing grueling work while isolated in the ocean.

But it was the loss of freedom I grieved.

It was still worth it. *She* was still worth it.

I'd spent the last nine years of my life on that rig. I made sure to work three times as hard as the next guy to prove that I was worthy. I didn't want to be known as the trust fund motherfucker with too much cashflow to have a lick of sense. I had something to prove, and over time, everyone grew to respect me and my work ethic. I never missed a day, never was late. I wasn't really friends with any of my coworkers, but we got along fine because there was a mutual respect shared between us.

We sweat. We clocked in, we clocked out, we spent weeks at a time secluded from the rest of the world, and we brought home a check once a month. It was honest work—the complete opposite of what my father expected of me—the complete opposite of what every Beauregard in history had done. I earned something. I did something. I didn't have to scheme for my job and for the six thousand dollars a month I earned. No, I just worked. Something my fucking brother knew nothing about.

And all of that was gone now.

Because Vera Garner called me, and I was fucked up in the head about it.

There was a lot of shit in my life that I didn't take seriously. I drank too much. I'd fucked enough women in various public places. I ruined people. I ruined relationships. My job was one of the few things I'd done right. And now? I'd do right by Vera, too.

From a distance.

I'd arrived at my father's home late in the evening almost exactly twenty-four hours after talking to Vera.

My girl.

My fucking girl. Mine to protect. Mine to fuck. Mine to love. Mine to keep away from all the bullshit of the Beauregard name. My possessiveness needed to take the back seat, but I refused to let this family ruin her like it did me.

When she called last night, I thought she was trying to get back together with me. But when I figured out she was with Jack? I knew shit wasn't right. She wasn't offering forgiveness, she was choking on her words and wrapped up with puppet strings. Even if I couldn't have her, there was no way in hell I'd let her be used.

I let myself into the front door, and a wave of

toxic familiarity washed over me. I both loved and hated this home.

It was the place mom loved most.

It was the place I saw Vera for the first time.

It was the place where Joseph abused me.

It was the place I found my mother's dead body.

"Jack?" I called out. "Where are you?" I took a few steps into the living room, my eyes trained on every inch I could see as I waited for someone to answer. "Jack!"

A small hand wrapped around my forearm, jerking me around. I spun to face who'd grabbed me. I was on a warpath. Getting that call from Vera had flipped me upside down. Why was she with Jack? What kind of fucked up arrangement did they have?

And why did I feel betrayed?

I needed to push her away, but first, I'd make sure she was okay.

But I couldn't do any of those things, because it wasn't Vera who grabbed me. It was her mother, Lilah. "Where is Vera?" I asked, my voice a growl.

"Away from here," she hissed before dragging me down the hall and away from the living room. She was so tiny, her grip so weak, but I allowed her to pull me away because I had a ton of fucking questions. I didn't like Lilah, and after witnessing firsthand how narcissistic she was toward her daughter, I didn't feel bad for hating the bitch.

"Where is Vera?" I asked again once we were in the hallway. I pulled out of her grip and took in the bags under her eyes and her hollowed cheeks. Why did she look so frail? Was that what I looked like every time Joseph had beaten the shit out of me?

"At her apartment, hopefully," she whispered while looking around, as if her husband would jump out of the shadows and attack her at any moment. Seeing Lilah so scared, so fragile, just emboldened my resolve to save Vera. I couldn't imagine seeing my girl as broken as her mother. I just had to do this delicately.

"Why are you acting shady as fuck right now?" I asked. I didn't have time to play her games.

"Because I overheard your little call last night," she spat in a low whisper. "I heard what you said to my daughter, you bastard."

I should have been ashamed, but I didn't give a fuck. I did what I had to do. Vera needed to move on. It was for her own good, even if it was the most fucking painful thing I'd ever done.

"What do you care?" I asked.

"I overheard Jack saying something about a deal they made to keep me safe. I don't like it."

That caught my attention. "What kind of deal?"

"I don't know, but Jack is up to something, okay? Maybe if you talk to him and end this, I can go back to my husband and Vera can be left alone. You don't want my daughter bothering you. I don't want her interfering in my marriage. Maybe if you figure out what Jack wants..."

My shoulders dropped. Of fucking course, she was only worried about herself and Joseph. "You don't care about your daughter, you just want to go back to DC," I said while looking her up and down.

"My daughter just doesn't understand..."

"I think she understands more than you know," I snapped.

Lilah's eyes widened. "I'll do anything, you know," she said before placing a hand on my chest. Her eyes became hooded with lust, and I nearly puked all over her. It was obvious just what she was insinuating. Bitch.

"Yeah, if I don't wanna fuck your daughter, I sure as fuck don't wanna fuck you. Back off." I moved out of her reach and considered my options.

"Hamilton? What are you doing here?" Jack interrupted. Lilah and I both spun around to face him, my stomach dropping at the sight of my father in a suit with his arms crossed over his chest. "The front guards said you'd arrived. I wasn't expecting to find you chatting with your sister-in-law. I was under the impression that the two of you didn't get along."

"We have a common interest," I growled.

"I assume you're talking about Vera, yes? She *is* lovely. I was thinking of ordering dinner. Should we invite her over?"

"Absolutely not. What's going on?" No wasting time, no dancing around the truth with games and bullshit.

Jack looked at me, then at Lilah. I didn't care about her. I didn't give two fucks that she wanted to go back to her husband and pretend like she wasn't getting the shit beat out of her. I was done with the games. I was exhausted and wanted to hop back on my bike and go to wherever Vera was. "I don't know what you mean," he said.

"What agreement do you have with Vera?" I asked, making my father smile.

"So you *do* care about her," he replied.

"I don't want anyone making deals involving me."

"Let's sit down and chat, shall we? I think all of this is a misunderstanding."

I took a step closer to my father. "I think *you're*

the one misunderstanding. I want answers, now. I don't appreciate you using Vera to get to me."

Jack frowned. "Fine. Let's talk. I actually have a proposition for you."

"Unless that proposition involves shoving a boot up my brother's ass and leaving this family for good, I'm not interested." I crossed my arms over my chest, feigning cool indifference.

Jack's lip twitched. "It involves your brother and protecting Vera," he said easily. I should have known this was coming. All this time, we worried that the Beauregard reputation was the biggest threat to a relationship between us. I never imagined that Jack would use Vera to get whatever he wanted from me. And that was the fucked-up part about all of this: I would do anything. Anyfuckingthing. I would sell my soul to the devil and sit alongside Jack if it meant keeping her safe.

"Let's talk," I agreed.

Jack didn't smile, but I saw how his eyes danced playfully; he was like a card shark with a superior hand. "If you'll excuse us, Lilah. This is a private conversation."

Lilah licked her lips before meekly nodding and walking away. Coward. If someone was fucking with my daughter, I'd do everything in my power to protect her. Lilah didn't deserve Vera.

I followed my father into his study. Jack found his recliner and a glass of whiskey. I leaned against the wall, eager to flee.

"Aren't you supposed to be on the rig?" Jack asked, opening up the conversation. It pissed me off that he knew my work schedule. "I'm assuming you no longer work there?"

"Don't bother making assumptions about my life. What do you want?"

"I was hoping we could have a pleasant conversation, but it seems you're eager to cut to the chase. I want you to work at Beauregard Industries. We have a unique cash flow problem I need investigated, but I don't necessarily trust anyone outside of this room to look into it."

Figures. Looking into cash flow problems was just a polite way of saying there were possibly some illegal activities. "What kind of problem?"

"A laundering problem."

"You're laundering money?" I asked. It seemed on brand. My father was corrupt. The only reason he got into politics was to create laws that made it easier for him to make more money.

"No. Of course not. But I think Joseph is."

I rolled my eyes. "I doubt you have nothing to do with this. But I'll play along. How do you figure?"

"You of all people know what he's capable of. This could be very bad."

I gritted my teeth before responding. "You *also* know what he's capable of, you just choose to turn a blind eye to it. What the fuck does this have to do with me? You know the ins and outs. I don't even have a college degree. Hell, I don't even know how many corporations you have your greedy fingers in these days."

"You know I like to keep my investments diverse," Jack replied before slowly taking a sip of his drink. I watched his Adam's apple move as he swallowed, and I had to fight the urge to stab him in the jugular. "And no one else can handle this. We have to keep this under lock and key, Hamilton. If I start digging around, Joseph will get suspicious, and I'm worried his reaction won't be good. If I tell him you decided to stop working on the rig and join the family business, it'll be less obvious. He knows I've been trying to get you more involved. Joseph underestimates you. He'd expect me to give you some bullshit job with a cushy role."

"Even if I did this, he wouldn't buy it. I've never

shown an interest in your work. The politics, the fortune. All of it."

"Well, I suppose we'll have to convince him otherwise. Perhaps you have a reason to want to climb the corporate ladder now? A certain girl you want to take care of? I'm sure we could find a reasonable explanation for your sudden interest in Beauregard Industries. I'm trying to keep this family from going to prison."

I scoffed. "You're trying to keep *yourself* out of prison. You don't care about me. I'm not helping you. Let's just get to the part where you blackmail me into getting what you want."

Jack huffed. "I don't want to blackmail you, Hamilton. I want us to work together to bring your brother down because he's out of control."

"I'm still not convinced. Explain what's going on. Why do you think there is laundering?"

My father took another sip of his drink before continuing. "Basically, there are large sums of money I can't account for in a few of my companies. There is a complex audit trail and a series of financial transactions that don't make sense. I think Joseph has some illegal capital, and he's using Beauregard Industries as a front to move funds around. One of my accountants brought it to my attention the night before Joseph's wedding. We were going to assemble a team and research the odd transactions, but she was in a tragic yet peculiar car accident four days later."

I swallowed. There was so much to dissect in his statement that I didn't even know where to start. What did he mean by *a peculiar car accident*? "Do you think Joseph killed her?" I asked, my blood like ice.

"I think he's involved with people capable of that. The IRS is constantly breathing down our necks, and something like this is usually caught in audits. It's peculiar. I have some of my best men and women working it out, but we're all coming up short. Whoever Joseph is in business with is damn good at what they do and has very high connections. I need to get to the source of it all before it's too late."

"What kind of illegal shit is Joseph into?" I asked while thinking of the drugs he used to do.

"Could be drugs again. Or it could be weapons. Human trafficking. I seriously have no idea," Jack said.

"That's seriously fucked up, Jack. Sounds to me like you have more problems than just your business being used to funnel illegal activities. Why don't you go to the cops with your findings and let them handle it?" I curled my lip while looking down at my weak father. He was so wrapped up in his own corruption that he didn't know right from wrong.

"Joseph is sloppy. Killing my accountant? And these funds are astronomical. I'm surprised I haven't been flagged yet. I just want to save our legacy, Hamilton."

"And I want nothing to do with this bullshit. If you're truly innocent, let the feds handle it."

My father let out a harsh exhale. "I don't want, nor do I need, an investigation, Hamilton."

So there was more going on? Dear old dad had too many skeletons in his closet. "I don't want, nor do I need, to be involved," I echoed.

Jack slammed his fist on the table, and I flinched, my triggers flooding to the surface of my consciousness with a vengeance. Joseph looked so much like our father. I stood up and straightened my spine, preparing for his rebuttal and aggression. "You will help me. Because there will be consequences if you don't. And because you can't resist bringing your brother down."

Consequences? Jack didn't know the meaning of the word. I'd burn down his house while he sleeps inside of it and spend the rest of my life in prison with a smile on my face.

Jack steadied his breathing and tilted his chin up.

"Vera could have a very good life, you know. She loves her school. Her classes. Her apartment. She's set up to have a nice career. The only thing holding her back really is her mother." I didn't want to be interested in what Jack was saying, but still I leaned closer to hear him better.

"Spit it out already, Jack. I'm bored with this."

"I know you care about her. You wouldn't be here right now if you didn't. You can push her away, but I know you. I know how far you're willing to go for the people you love."

Cruel. My father was cruel for reminding me of that gruesome moment. The foam in her mouth. My burning, aching muscles as I tried to bring her back.

"Fuck you," I growled.

My father wasn't bothered by my words. "I'll give her the world. I'll keep her away from Joseph and me. I'll encourage Joseph to divorce Lilah and provide the two of them with a nice settlement. I'll never talk to her again, and she can go back to living her life, going to school, and staying out of Beauregard business."

My mouth dried. His offer was tempting. "Don't act like getting rid of Vera and Lilah is such a sacrifice," I spat. "It's obvious you hate Lilah."

Jack's eyes went glassy. "It's curious how she

managed to raise such a selfless, compassionate daughter." He took another sip of his whiskey. "And yes. It wouldn't be much of a hardship on my part, but something tells me that it would mean much more to you."

He wasn't wrong. I wanted Vera out of this. I wanted her far away from the Beauregard bullshit, especially if Joseph was dealing with some top shelf criminal activity.

"Vera is more than capable of getting out on her own if she wants to," I replied.

Jack shrugged. "Couldn't hurt to shove her in the right direction, though, no?"

"Tell me about your arrangement with her," I pressed. If I were being honest, it still pissed me off that Vera was even working with him. She didn't owe me anything, but I thought she was smarter than that.

"I've been trying to get you into the fold for years, Hamilton. I figured Vera would help motivate you to at least try and have a relationship with me."

"And she agreed to this?" I asked in disbelief.

"Of course she did. I held her tuition and her mother's safety over her head."

I pressed my lips into a thin line and mulled over his words. I was pissed that Jack was holding this shit over her head. Pissed that she agreed to this bullshit plan. Didn't she know me by now? Didn't she know that I'd see through the bullshit and call her out?

I wanted to punish her for even thinking this could work. I wanted to save her from my asshole father, too. The conflict raging inside of me pissed me right the fuck off. "I'm still not convinced."

Jack huffed. "You've spent your entire life trying to bring down your brother. You tried setting up a scandal just to tarnish his name. I've had to fight you tooth and nail your entire life, and now that I'm finally giving you what you want, you don't want to do it?"

I averted my eyes and shifted from one foot to the other. "Forgive me for not believing that you'd want anything to happen to your precious son."

"You're my son, too, Hamilton," Jack quickly replied. "I know I've ignored you in the past. I'm so sorry. You didn't deserve what you went through, and I want to make it right. Together. We can bring Joseph down for his careless, cruel behavior. Everyone wins."

I despised the way my chest warmed with Jack's words. All I'd ever wanted, my entire life, was to feel accepted by him. So many times, I begged him to do something about Joseph. Could this really be my chance to bring him down for good?

"I'll help you—guide you every step of the way," he promised. "We never got the chance to bond. I want to do this with you, Hamilton."

"What kind of things do you need to know?" I asked. I wasn't committing to this, but I needed all the information to make a decision. Jack grinned slightly.

"Anything you can give me. I just want to find out exactly what Joseph is doing so we can shut it down before the feds find out. I want to save our legacy and put you in a position to lead our company. I'm getting old, Hamilton. I want you involved in the family business."

"I never wanted to be involved," I whispered.

Jack popped his knuckles. "You can't avoid what you're born into," he stated ominously.

His words were simple but felt damning. Being born into something unavoidable was a universal truth that bonded Vera and me. "I'm not sure—"

Jack frowned. "Joseph is out of control. We have to stop him before it's too late. Don't you want revenge?"

I let out a bitter laugh. "He's been out of control since I was born. He was out of control when he broke my arm. He was also out of control when he beat his wife. But God forbid he fuck with your money, right, dad?"

"If we're audited, everyone is going to prison," Jack sputtered. "Including Lilah."

Fuck. "Why Lilah? The way I see it, you and Joseph are the only people taking the fall when shit goes south. And what makes you think I care if you get arrested?" I asked.

"You care because you love Vera," Jack answered. His statement rang true but felt like a curse pouring from his lips. "And Lilah has been with Joseph the most these last few months. I'm keeping her here so I can figure out if she has any useful information. I'm willing to bet she's involved somehow. You know Vera would be devastated if her mother got arrested. I can protect Lilah," he insisted.

"What would you have me do?"

"Find proof of the laundering. I'm slowly removing Joseph from accounts. Get close to your brother. Make amends so you can figure out what the hell he's doing. Let's end this once and for all."

"You want me to be a detective," I said with a laugh.

"I want you to be a Beauregard!" Jack yelled, the veins bulging in his neck. "I trusted the wrong son, and now he's on the verge of ruining everything. I want you to be a man, Hamilton. I want you to let go of your grudge and do what needs to be done. You've been working with Saint to bring down your brother, you've been doing everything in your power to ruin our reputation, and now that I'm handing you an opportunity on a silver platter, you're going to turn it down?"

I stared at Jack.

I trusted the wrong son.

I trusted the wrong son.

"I'm not such a bastard anymore, am I?" I asked bitterly. "Guess you only love people that you need."

"You were never a bastard, Hamilton. I'll protect Vera. I'll make sure she's far away from this. I'll continue to pay for her schooling. Her apartment. I'll make sure she has everything she needs. I'll make sure she's safe and happy. Joseph will never lay a hand on her. But you're going to step up. You're going to end this."

"I don't even know what I'm looking for. I'm not qualified."

"I'll help you."

I laughed. "You're incapable of helping me."

"I'll tell you what to look for. You're smarter than you give yourself credit for, Hamilton."

I didn't trust him. I didn't trust this plan for a single second. And yet...

I couldn't believe I was considering this. "How long will it take?"

"However long it takes," Jack replied. "Something of this magnitude could take a year. Maybe two. We need to find the source of the illegal cash flow, flush out the criminals working with Joseph, and find evidence incriminating him. I can have the private jet take you to DC in an hour and divorce papers delivered to Lilah by tomorrow."

A year without Vera. Was that even possible? It would have to be. I'd be spending the rest of my life without her.

I didn't want to be in DC with my brother. I didn't want to be away from Vera. But being closer to him meant I'd have more opportunities to figure out what the fuck he's up to. I was so fucking pissed. I felt out of control of my own life but determined to fix this. Jack knew exactly how to get me under his thumb.

"I need a couple of days to think," I said.

"We don't have a couple of days," Jack snapped.

I just wanted to see Vera one last time. Even though I'd already decided to end this, I needed one last moment with my girl. I needed to hold her. Fuck her until she couldn't walk for a year. Burn my memory so deeply into her mind that she didn't go a single day without thinking of me too.

"Give me a couple days," I replied. "If you want me to do this, then you can be patient."

Jack sighed. "Fine," he said.

4

VERA

*A*n invisible force animated my heart, like jump-starting my mother's old car. After sitting alone in my apartment for hours, the harsh sound of someone knocking on my door boomed around me. A startling resurrection out of my somber thoughts. I recognized the assuming power behind it almost instantly. Hamilton's voice cut through my deadbolted front door and slithered across my skin.

I sat up on my couch and touched my lips with the tips of my fingertips.

"Open the door, Petal."

The demand was swift. Painful. I padded across the hardwood floors of my apartment, not caring that I hadn't showered since leaving Jack's house. Not caring that my thin tank top had coffee stains on the strap. Goose bumps broke out on my legs as I unlocked the door. It was close to midnight, and I'd spent all day crying over the cruel things Hamilton had said to me. I wasn't sure if I was capable of enduring that again. How could I keep protecting my mother if Hamilton wanted nothing to do with me?

I didn't crack open the door, I swung it wide open. I'm sure there was a metaphor for the way I felt about Hamilton hidden in that single move, but it'd be a waste to analyze it. I couldn't even begin to tell you why I still cared for this man—why I ached for him in such a devastating way. Was I just a pathetic girl pining for an unattainable man?

Despite his cruel words still ringing in my mind, the moment Hamilton came into view, a sense of belonging settled over me. He looked strung out. His bloodshot eyes raked up and down my exposed skin as he ran a hand through his wild hair. The black pants on his long legs were ripped at the knee. He had on a white V-neck shirt with the collar stretched out. The dark circles under his eyes gave me some relief. Misery loves company.

"What are you doing here?" I asked while wrapping my arms around myself. The cool air hit my exposed skin. He reached for my wrists and stopped me from using my limbs as a shield. Jerking me forward, he forced my arms around his muscular frame and wrapped me in a bone crushing hug. "Stop," I demanded. "Let go."

I had to at least pretend to not want the comfort he offered.

"I'm going to hurt you again, Petal," he admitted ominously before kissing the top of my head and shuddering. I didn't think it was possible to hurt me more than he already did.

I once knew this girl that got bitten by a brown recluse spider. Everyone in our fifth grade class sent her cards in the hospital. For months, that invincible venom burned through her veins. She almost lost her leg. No matter how hard they tried, they just couldn't get the open wound to heal. I couldn't help but think about how Hamilton's betrayal was still a festering sore blooming on my heart, and his words were like a spider bite that refused to scab over. It would always be there. Always remind me of the vengeful enemy that got the last word. But, God, my heart still beat for him. Every pounding hit of my pulse was a painful reminder that I loved this man.

"You came here to hurt me?" I asked in confusion while finally pulling out of his hold. The man was full of melodramatic comments and riddles. "You already spoke your piece. I get it. We're done. You don't have to—"

"How are you?"

His question made me pause. "How am I? Just yesterday you told me my pussy was used up and that you wanted nothing to do with me—"

Hamilton kissed me. Dark and desperate, his soft lips pressed against mine without warning. Kissing Hamilton was vicious and haunting. Hard and ruining. Forgetting how much he'd hurt me, I pathetically wrapped my arms around his neck and lavished his mouth with my own, all while ignoring that small, intrusive thought that this was wrong.

It was a privilege to kiss Hamilton Beauregard. It wasn't wholesome, like the tender moments shared between two lovers. It wasn't kind or polite.

Kissing him was like a glorious apology. A physical manifestation of the truth budding between us. Sweeping tongues. Crashing teeth. Sucking. Groaning. He tugged on my lip. I pulled at his soul.

But maybe this was his version of trying? Maybe he'd realized he still wanted me? Maybe this could work after all, and Jack...

His father.

I broke our kiss, and Hamilton groaned while digging his fingers into my back, holding me in place as I looked up into his black eyes. "Is this another trick?" I asked. "Is this because I was with Jack yesterday? Some revenge ploy to show how desperate I am?" I put more space between us.

His eyes softened. "Yeah. I know you were with Jack," he said. "Can we not talk about it for a little while? Can I just be with you?"

My mind spiraled, and my mouth quickly followed suit. Words spilled from me like vomit. "But are you with me, Hamilton? We've been through so much. I'm still hurt by what you did, and now with what you said. We can't go back from that. I can't believe I kissed you just now. I'm so fucking stupid. How desperate can I get? I mean, seriously. You were wrong for me before, but now you're bad for me, too. Why are you even here?"

I looked down at the ground, but Hamilton didn't let me stare off for long. He placed his finger under my chin and forced me to look up at me. "I know about your arrangement with Jack."

"You do?" I asked, my voice barely a whisper.

"I'm going to help you, Petal. I'm going to chat with Jack and make sure your mother is safe. I'll help you keep your end of the deal."

How did he know? "Wh-why?"

Hamilton gripped my hips and started walking me backward toward the couch. He sat down with a thud and pulled me on top of him. My sleep shorts were too thin, barely covering my round ass as I straddled him. "Sit here," he instructed. I obeyed, dumbfounded.

"Why?" I asked again. "Why did you say those things to me yesterday if you were just going to help me today?"

"I say stupid shit all the time."

I rolled my eyes. "Don't downplay the things you said. It hurt me. You hurt me."

Hamilton stiffened. "I'm sorry, Petal," he said. "I didn't mean it. I didn't mean any of it. I just..." He shook his head, never finishing his statement. His hands drifted up under my tank, brushing along the edge of my ribs. My breath hitched. "Let me help you, Petal." Normally, the request would sound playful coming from Hamilton Beauregard's lips, but this sounded like a plea—him begging for me right here, right now. "I can clear your mind. Make you forget all the awful things I said."

"Maybe I don't want to forget. And you don't clear my mind, you take it over completely," I admitted. "When it's you and me, I can't think of anything else..." Hamilton lifted up a little, pressing his hard cock against my center.

"I like you best when you're only thinking of me," he admitted.

I pressed my forehead to his. "Stop talking in circles and spouting bullshit. Are you using me right now, Hamilton? What's going on?" This felt like a trick.

"Petal," he whispered. "I just want to be with you like this one more time."

The hair stood up on the back of my neck. It was a shock to the system, like getting struck with lightning. "What? What do you mean *one more time*?" I pulled away, standing up on shaky legs as I stared down at him. "I don't understand."

"I'm going to help you, Vera. I just want one last time with you. Everything will be taken care of. Your mom will never have to see Joseph again. I just want you to give me a goodbye. I want to love you one more time."

My brows rose up. My mouth dropped open. I thought we'd already said goodbye. When I found out Saint was his brother, I ended things, but there was a little something in the back of my mind, a hint of hope that made it not feel over.

"Goodbye?" I asked.

"We both always knew it would end, Petal."

"Stop calling me that. What the fuck is up with this whiplash, Hamilton? Yesterday, you wanted nothing to do with me. Now you want to love and leave me?" Hamilton stood up and sauntered closer to me. I backed away, keeping out of his reach, though he stalked me like a predator. I propped a hand on my hip. "How exactly did you think this was going to work? One last goodbye fuck in exchange for keeping Jack's end of the deal? That doesn't even make sense."

"Petal, I'm sorry," he said.

I placed both hands on my skull and squeezed. "You're making me crazy," I cried out. "I feel so fucking stupid. Why are you doing this to me? Why couldn't you just leave me alone, Hamilton? Why do you have to draw this out like this?"

"You're the one that made a deal with Jack," he growled. "You're the one that put me in this position. I figure I owe you one for the article with Saint. You want out? I'll get you out. But I want something for it. I don't want you calling me for Jack. I don't want to deal with his bullshit games. All you have to do is this. Right now. One last goodbye. Tell me you don't want one more time with me and I'll leave. We had great chemistry, Petal. Why not benefit from Jack's deal?"

"You hate Jack. Why would you do this? I doubt it's just because you want to get your dick wet."

Hamilton scowled. "You're right."

"There's something going on. You obviously still care about me, or you wouldn't be here," I pressed. "But still you want some toxic goodbye sex?"

"Why do you have to pick this apart?!" he yelled.

I shook my head and slumped my shoulders. "You hurt me," I said. "Hamilton, I don't deserve this. It's not right. You betrayed me in the worst possible way. You lied to me our entire relationship—if you could even call it that. And then you just let me go. You didn't care enough about me to fight for us. And when I called? You said some pretty cruel things. I haven't even had time to process everything that's happened, and now you want a quick fuck? And even worse, you're bargaining with my mother's safety. I thought you were better than that." I swallowed the emotion rising up my throat before continuing. "You're pushing me away, and I don't know why. But I do know that it's not my job to chase after you. I've spent my entire life begging to be loved. And you know what? You made me realize that it's not enough. I could have loved you, Hamilton. Fiercely."

"Petal. I can't..." Hamilton's face was twisted up with pain. But it didn't make a difference. Can't. Won't. It was all the same.

"You want to walk away? Well, fuck that. I walked away first. I walked away when you lied to me and used me. You can see yourself out."

He looked up and glared at me, fire in his eyes as he clenched and unclenched his fists at his side. "I want a goodbye, Petal."

"Well, you don't get one!" I screamed. "Get out."

He ignored me and walked forward. I stepped backward. I wanted him out of here. My back collided with the wall. A shelf holding a framed photo of my mother and me at the wedding crashed down to the ground. Glass shattered everywhere and crunched under Hamilton's boot as he continued to move closer to me.

Shards were scattered around my bare feet, and once we were face-to-face, he swept me up and cradled me to his chest. "Let me down!"

"Don't want you to cut yourself, Petal," he purred before walking me to my bedroom and kicking the door open. Tears started to fill my eyes, and those annoying insecurities that plagued me filled my mind. Was I not good enough? When given the choice, Hamilton didn't choose me. I suppose it was better than having no choice at all.

Maybe I could give him this last goodbye. Maybe it would be the closure I needed. It was like breathing with a blade in your side. Every inhale was sharp, but fuck, I was breathing.

"Please give me this. I know it's shit. Everyone takes from you, and I'm a selfish bastard for asking. Just let me kiss you, Petal," he urged while laying me down on the bed and crawling to hover over me. I swatted at the hot tears flowing down my cheeks. He kissed every single droplet. His hands found the edge of my shorts, and he pulled them down. I had a moment, when our eyes connected. I took in the question in his glassy stare and drowned in a puddle of self-pity that quickly morphed into rage.

"You want a goodbye, Hamilton?" I asked as the pain in my chest cracked and all the disappointment flowed out with a vengeance. What even was the truth anymore? Did he care about me? Did he think I wasn't worth the effort?

He clenched his teeth, the move making his defined jaw harden into a sharp line. "Are you going to give it to me?"

"And you'll help with Jack?" I asked.

His eyes flashed with rage. "As long as I never see your face again, I'll make sure Jack's agreement is met."

My heart cracked. I felt cheap. Used. I was done. Done with all of it. Done with the Beauregards. Done with the blackmail. Done with my mother's guilt. My insecurities. I was done with him.

Hamilton then choked out words that softened the blow. "I want you to live your life, Petal. I want you to be happy without me."

I wrapped my legs around his middle and rolled us both over. Pressing him into the mattress, I shrugged out of my sleep tank and clawed at the soft fabric of his shirt. He quickly tore it from his body while kicking his boots off to the ground. "Fuck you, Hamilton," I whispered before scraping my teeth along his chest. I savored him. I fought with him. My fingers undid the button to his pants, and he slid them down.

"Love you too, Petal," he said in a reverent tone, his voice so soft that I almost didn't hear it. It was the most tender sound. "I bet you're drenched. You still want me. Even when I hurt you, your pussy aches for me."

Shame filled me. This was some sick kink for Hamilton. He liked knowing he could still have my body after destroying my heart. I raged.

I groaned. "I want your cock. I want your goodbye. I want to get off so I can kick you out of my apartment and out of my life."

We undressed like each scrap of fabric between us was a weapon. He bucked, I pressed him into the mattress. I lined up my sex with his and watched his lips part as I slowly slid down and began riding him. With him fully inside me, he groaned low and slow. I bent over to whisper in his ear. "Enjoy it while you can, because I'm done."

Hamilton tensed, then grabbed my hips. He guided my movements, but it wasn't enough. Flipping me back over onto my stomach, he pulled my long brown hair and started pounding into me relentlessly from behind. His thick cock felt like a blissful punishment. I arched my back and propped myself up as he reached around to furiously rub my clit in perfectly timed circles with just enough pressure to send me over the edge.

I preferred this position. I didn't have to look him in the eye as he commanded my body to come. I didn't have to see his expression as he moaned and grunted. I was just a body, I was just something he used in the dead of night to get off to. I felt him thrust in and out. Harder, harder, harder. The nasty sounds of our skin slapping filled my bedroom.

He pulled out and laid down on the mattress, facing me. "You going to come or what?" I asked bitterly. I already wanted him gone. He turned me, forcing our bodies to face one another as he grabbed my thigh and pulled it over his hip. He thrust inside of me once more. We were so impossibly close. I could feel him deep in my soul as he fucked me.

"Hurry up and get off, Hamilton," I moaned.

"Don't fucking rush me," he growled with a curse before wrapping his hand around my throat. He squeezed until I couldn't breathe. He hit just the right amount of pressure to make me forget. The fight fled from my body, and I felt my pulse slow. I let darkness cloud the edges of my vision. He released and another orgasm made my entire body shudder. I cried out as he pumped me steadily. His lips found mine, swallowing my pleasure like it was a tasty treat. Emotions wrecked me.

"Hamilton," I begged, I sobbed.

Hamilton came.

He pulled out.

He stared at me.

He got up.

He got dressed, his dick still coated with our combined pleasure.

He paused at the door, looked at me with sad eyes and spoke words that would haunt me for months. "I just want you to be happy, Petal. And I'm not capable of doing that."

Then, he walked out of my bedroom.

He walked out of the front door.

And he walked out of my life.

*J*ack's house looked oddly serene as I pulled up the long, winding drive. Light sliced through the clouds, illuminating the clean landscaping. Despite the fall weather, not a single leaf littered the lawn. It looked so perfectly Beauregard. I wanted to take a can of spray paint to the lawn so it more accurately represented the people who lived there. I could have dug trenches around the property with my dull fingernails.

I blinked my bloodshot eyes while nodding at the security guard at the gate. I'd spent most of the last couple of days in a numb haze. My mind had hit its threshold of pain, and there was nothing left for me to feel.

I let him fuck me. I let him use me up. Hamilton wanted goodbye sex, and I offered my body up on a silver platter. Love was like a pendulum, and I kept going back and forth, always stuck, never actually going anywhere.

Did I love myself at all?

In the moment, I convinced myself that it was all to protect my mother. I pretended like it was some grand sacrifice, some sick satisfaction. Just one last goodbye.

But I didn't do it for my mother. I let Hamilton use me up because I was addicted to him. I knew that we were through, and I wanted just one more night with him. One more time to feel full and desired. I let myself be burdened with the memory of him because it was better than having no memory at all.

Fucking pathetic. Stupid. Why do I always do this to myself?

Pick my petals, world.

It was pitiful, and I could barely look at myself in the mirror, let alone attend classes this week. I hated the power he held over me. Hell, I hated how much power everyone seemed to hold over me. I let him take over my mind, my body, and my ability to function. I let my mother's happiness and safety supersede my own. And for what?

I parked the car and gripped the steering wheel, my knuckles white from how hard I was grabbing it. I didn't want to be here. I wasn't in the mood to talk to my selfish mother, but when she sent an urgent text demanding I go to Jack's house right away, I obeyed. I was chronically obedient. Pathetic. Lame.

I walked up the steps leading to Jack's home and debated between knocking on the door and just walking inside. It was so strange, not being able to discern where I stood with this family. I hated the uncertainties.

Before I could decide, the front door was ripped open and my sobbing mother threw herself at me. The drama. The poised theatrics nearly tipped me over. I caught her—barely. And she went limp in my arms. What the fuck had happened? Who died?

"Mom?" I said in confusion. "What's going on? Is Joseph here?"

She pulled away from me and scowled. "No," she spat. "He isn't here. He'll never be here. It's like he was never really here, huh? Gone. Just gone!" She let out a screech before continuing. What the fuck? "He couldn't be bothered to deliver the news to me in person." She ran her long nails into my skin. I helped her stand back up while processing her words.

I looked at my mother, with her crazed expression and baggy clothes barely hanging onto her thin frame. Her hair was a wild mess of waves, and she ran her trembling hand through her highlighted tresses while staring past me and at the winding drive.

"What are you talking about?" I asked.

"He's divorcing me, Vera. Joseph had the papers delivered this morning," she wailed before hunching over and letting out a painful sob. "Not even a text. Not a call. Just a man with a briefcase."

My initial instinct was to fist pump the air and thank God. Getting my mother as far away from her abusive husband as possible was my number one priority. If he didn't want her anymore, then we were free to get the hell away from here. Was this Jack's doing? Hamilton's? He promised me that he would take care of things.

Even though I was excited, I knew that I needed to tread lightly. It took considerable effort to hide the smile on my face. "I'm so sorry, Mom," I said softly, and even though I wasn't sorry that Joseph was gone, I meant it. I was sorry for her heartbreak. I was sorry that she had to go through this. I was sorry that her first shot at love and normalcy turned out so bleak.

She wasn't completely innocent, and she absolutely dug her own grave by lying about the pregnancy, but that didn't mean I couldn't sympathize with her pain. Heartbreak was something that bonded us, ironically. "Did he tell you why?" I asked.

Mom's beady eyes snapped to me, her lips curled into a snarl, and she cocked her head to the side. "You know why."

Mom poked me in the chest with her index finger, and I gaped at her, not quite understanding what she meant. "What? Mom, let's go sit down. Where is Jack?"

"This is your fault. You couldn't stand me having this one thing, so you had to go and ruin it!" She poked at me again, this time harder. I rubbed the spot where she dug her index finger into my chest and frowned. "You dated Hamilton. You called Jack and made some sort of arrangement to get me here. You wanted this."

"I didn't want this!" I argued.

"Oh? You never wanted me to marry him. Admit it."

I sighed. "It was a rushed marriage, yes, but all I ever wanted was your happine—"

"You just want me to be miserable!"

Yes, I wanted this, but at the end of the day, ending a marriage was Joseph's decision. He was a grown man. I didn't force him to draft up divorce papers and serve them to my mother. "This is not my fault," I argued. "Joseph is capable of making his own decisions. Yes, I wanted you to be safe, and I went to Jack when I was concerned for your health and well-being, but, Mom, I'm not responsible for Joseph wanting to end your marriage. It's not fair to put that on me."

Mom tilted her head back and laughed in such a manic way that my eyes widened in shock. She then doubled over, as if the humor of my words were so funny that she had to grab her stomach to hold in the belly laughs. "Not fair?" she asked while wiping tears from her eyes with the side of her index finger. "Not fair? What's not fair is raising an ungrateful daughter that ruins EVERYTHING!"

I took a step back. Mom was hurting, but there was no excuse for her hurtful words. Maybe it was the residual pain of Hamilton using me, or maybe I was just fed up with being blamed for every bad thing that happened to my mother.

No. Not today. Not anymore.

"What's not fair is you lying about a pregnancy to trap Joseph in a loveless marriage," I started before poking her in the chest, mimicking the toxic way she tried to hurt me. "What's not fair is having a mother that blames you for fucking existing." I poked her again, and we both stepped inside the house. "What's not fair is being treated like an accessory. What's not fair is having a narcissistic, gaslighting mother who can't take responsibility for her own failed marriage to a monster." Mom gaped at me, and I kept going. "You treat me like a burden, and I am sick of it. All I've ever done is care for you. I won't apologize for trying to save your damn life."

"How dare you! I just found out I'm getting a divorce, and your first reaction is to attack me?!" she deflected.

"Only because your first reaction was to blame me for your failed marriage! Get over yourself! I'm sorry you're hurting, Mom. I hate that you're going through this, but I can't stand here and let you blame me anymore. You're entitled to your feelings, but I'm not required to suffer because of them any longer. Do you even know what a healthy coping mechanism is? I'm your daughter. Not your friend, not your sister, and certainly not your mother. I'm your fucking daughter!"

I was screaming so loud that my throat burned. My chest heaved as I stared at the broken woman in front of me. I didn't feel an ounce of regret.

I felt free.

"Wow," I said to myself while nodding. Mom sobbed harder. "That felt really good."

"You don't care about me at all, you selfish little bitch," Mom spat.

"The apple doesn't fall far from the tree, Lilah!" I yelled before clasping my hand over my mouth in disbelief.

Since the moment Mom married Joseph, I'd been working up to this moment. Hamilton broke me down, and I was building myself back up. "I'm done," I said softly.

"You have everything, Vera! Everything. You got to go to school. You got to go to prom, to graduation—"

"Stop blaming me for having a different life than yours! You didn't have to keep me, Mom. I'm so thankful you did, but I'd rather be motherless than live a life where I have to apologize for existing."

"I loved you. I did everything for you," she sobbed.

"And I'm thankful for that, but you need to take a hard look at your life and how you treat me," I said. Calm, my tone was deadly calm. "I won't let you do this to me anymore. I'm done."

"What does that even mean? You can't quit family." Once again, she went to the extreme.

"I'm not quitting you. Stop going to such extremes, you narcissistic psycho. I'm done with being your verbal punching bag. I'm done with the guilt. I'm just...done. If you want to go back to being my mother and stop caring about all this materialistic bullshit, then you know where to find me."

"What is going on here?" Jack asked. His tie was undone, and the top button of his shirt flared open, revealing his chest. "Lilah, are you okay?"

Mom curled her hand into a fist and pressed it against her mouth before dramatically running over to Jack and falling into his open arms. "Joseph is leaving me, Jack. And Vera is being so cruel."

Jack looked oddly calm as he patted her back, as if he expected her to act this way. He probably knew about the divorce papers before all of us. "Vera, this is a really difficult time for your mother. I think all of us need to be patient and understanding right now."

Mom sniffled and pulled away from Jack. "What am I going to do? Where am I going to go? Oh, gosh. I can't stay here."

Jack reached out and grabbed her shoulder. "You can stay here as long as you need to. It's been nice having someone else in the house. Just because my son is an idiot doesn't mean I'll kick you out." Mom looked up at Jack like he was a prophet capable of healing childhood cancer. Her eyes widened. She blinked twice and licked her lips.

"You'll really let me stay here?" she asked, her voice a sensual rasp. I couldn't even believe what I was witnessing. Was my mom always this transparent and I just now realized it? Or had her life with Joseph twisted her up into this lying, scheming person?

"You can't be serious," I said in disbelief.

"Where else do you expect me to go?" Mom cried dramatically. "In fact, where do you think you're going? Jack and Joseph pay for your apartment and your tuition." She scoffed. "Not too high and mighty now, huh?"

A shot of fear went through me, but it was short-lived. I could handle this. I could figure my shit out. Get a job and—

"No one is going to be homeless. Just because the two of you didn't work out doesn't mean we can't find a way to make sure you're safe. I told Vera I would take care of her schooling and apartment until she graduated, and I have every intention of keeping that promise. Education is very important to me."

I looked at Jack for a moment. It all clicked into place. "Have you spoken to Hamilton?" I asked.

Mom clutched her chest. "Is everything always about Hamilton? What about me!?"

Jack ignored her. Politely, of course. Or at least as polite as he could be while pretending she wasn't making everything about her. "Hamilton and I had a really great chat. He came over, and I think we're going to finally have the fresh start I've always wanted. He made it clear that your relationship was over."

So Hamilton actually spoke to his father? Interesting. He hated Jack. If he was willing to actually go through with this, then...shit, maybe I was responsible for Joseph divorcing my mother. Hamilton had said we wouldn't have to worry about Joseph anymore. I just wasn't expecting everything to happen so quickly. Why was Hamilton doing this for me?

Why did I care?

I wanted out. This was my chance to walk away from all of it.

"I don't want your money," I blurted out.

Jack blanched. "What?"

"I never wanted to go to Greenwich University. I never wanted to live at your apartment or drive your cars or participate in your schemes." I looked at my mother. "You want someone to blame for your failed marriage? You're living with him. He's been looking for a reason to get rid of you since before you and Joseph were even married."

Mom gasped. Jack grinned and put his hands up defensively. "Now, Vera, please don't spread lies. Your mother has a lot to process. Why don't you go back to your apartment, and we can—"

"No," I said while rolling my shoulders back.

Jack looked at me in confusion. "What?"

I lifted my chin up. "No." I was over all of this. I was too raw to process or plan what my next move was, but I knew right here, right now, I was pulling myself out of this train wreck. I wasn't a Beauregard. I wasn't Lilah's daughter. I wasn't a fucking Rose or Petal or anything. I was my own motherfucking person, and nobody was going to fuck with me ever again.

"Call me if you want to have a real conversation about the dynamics of our relationship, Mom," I said before lifting the strap of my purse higher up on my shoulder and looking at Jack. "I'm going to borrow your car because Uber rates are astronomical," I said with a giggle while clapping my hands together. Was this what it felt like to stop caring? "I'll park it and mail you the keys. Have a nice life, Jack."

I spun on my heels and headed toward the door, with my mother's sobs ringing in my ear. It wasn't until I was on the front porch that I could have sworn I heard Hamilton's muffled voice in my mind, praising me for finally standing up for myself.

"That's my girl..."

"**Y**ou smell like a fucking bar, Hamilton," Jack growled as we walked down the street toward the hotel where my brother was staying. DC was booming with energy this morning. Men in suits pushed past us while talking on the phone, and tourists took pictures of my father as he kept a pristine smile on his face, despite being frustrated with me.

"Considering you plucked me from a barstool in

Greenwich last night, I suppose that's an accurate description," I stated coolly while smoothing my wrinkled shirt. I drank until the pain became mild, though it still burrowed deep. A constant presence that shamed me.

I spent all of yesterday and last night doing four things:

Mourning my relationship with Vera.

Learning about Beauregard Industries from Saint.

Hiding from my best friend—who would kick me in the balls for working with my dad.

Drinking my ass off.

My phone pinged, and I pulled it out of my pocket to check my messages. Hope flared to life within me. I felt like a delirious plane crash survivor trapped on an island, listening to the wind for another plane to save me, even though it was the same thing that stranded me in the first place. It was bullshit, but I partly hoped it was Vera reaching out. I wanted to talk to her. I wanted her to tell me that she'd done it—she'd finally told off her mother. She didn't know it, but I got a front row seat to the intense showdown. I was visiting my dad, hiding in the hallway when she told Lilah to grow the fuck up. It was beautiful. I wanted to kiss her in that moment, but then I remembered that I was the asshole pushing her away and hurting her over and over and over again. I pushed her away at her lowest point, so I sure as fuck didn't deserve her at her best.

Saint: Just landed in DC. Let me know when you can meet.

Saint was probably the last person I should be working with right now, but I trusted Jack about as far as I could throw him. Saint was blacklisted and eager to find a story to redeem his name. We made quite the pair. It felt like I was betraying Vera by going back to him, but I figured the sooner we could finish this shit, the sooner I could...

Well, I wasn't exactly sure what I was going to do once this was all over. Not knowing was very attractive to me. If I were to decide, then I'd have to deal with the possibility of never seeing Vera again.

"I shouldn't have trusted you with this. How can I be sure that you won't be getting drunk when you're supposed to be watching Joseph?"

I rolled my eyes. "We have to make this believable, Jack. Joseph expects me to be the dumb, destructive member of the family," I replied. I had drowned myself in enough whiskey to tranquilize a horse last night, so I was pretty prepared for my starring role. Jack and I left Connecticut at six o'clock this morning, barely giving me a chance to grab my dog and a backpack of clothes. The second we got off the plane, Jack signed papers for a rental house for me and had his assistant take Little Mama there.

"You look like shit. Keep a couple steps behind me," he snapped.

"You are such an encourager, Jack. I mean, really, you should write a book on parenting. I bet it would sell millions." Jack straightened his spine at my words, obviously agitated. "If you had given me more time, I probably would have showered and put on my other pair of ripped jeans."

Jack scoffed and halted at the front door of the hotel where Joseph was staying until his house was fully built. Of course, he couldn't do the normal thing and get himself an apartment. No, my brother had to get the penthouse suite. Two grand a night for the hotel staff to kiss his ass. It was the kind of waste of money that made me sick.

"Before we go up there, I need us to be on the same page. I'm going to explain to Joseph that you want to work—"

"Wrong," I interrupted before blowing a ceremonial raspberry to show Jack just how shitty that plan was. "That won't work."

Jack frowned before smoothing his sleek suit. "And why not?"

"Because you're starting off with that I want to be here. We both know that's a bold-faced lie. I don't want to be here. If you want to convince Joseph that I'm really here to work? Play to his ego and follow my lead." I mean, fuck, I thought Jack was a manipulative politician, didn't he know how to con a person? "But first," I said before grabbing his shoulder, halting him in his tracks. "Tell me about Vera."

Jack sighed. "Really? Right now?"

"Right now." I needed a little motivation to go up and deal with my brother.

"She slept at her apartment last night, but the doorman saw her leaving with a single suitcase and a backpack. She turned in her key and headed to school. This morning, I was refunded her tuition for next semester, so I'm assuming she isn't going to Greenwich University in the spring. I have people following her. She has a couple hundred bucks in her bank account. I might add some more—"

"No. Don't. She doesn't want your money."

To say I was surprised that Vera told her mother off would be an understatement. I was so fucking proud of her. If she wanted to go off on her own, then I supported that. But I wasn't afraid to get creative about helping her behind the scenes.

"She's probably going to go job hunting," I added while stroking my scruffy chin. "Have your people find out where she applies and make sure she gets it. With good pay."

Jack pulled out his phone and sighed. "Consider it done." I watched him type, pulling strings with a single press of a button.

"Good. I want her to feel like she's doing it all on her own. We'll just provide a little behind the scenes support."

"Whatever you say," Jack replied.

I yawned. "Great. Good talk. Let's go fuck with Joseph." I started marching inside the hotel, and he followed after me.

"I don't think you're sober enough to think this through rationally," Jack complained as we made our way through the lavish lobby and toward an elevator manned by one of those cheesy dudes with the round cap to press a fucking button for us, because God forbid, we press our own buttons.

"Trust me," I insisted. "You want me to trust you? It's give and take, Jack."

He huffed, and I didn't care. "I hate it when you call me that," he said in a soft voice.

"You hate your name?" I challenged, even though I knew what he meant. I'd been calling him Jack ever since Mom died.

He shook his head, not bothering to argue with me. "Let's get this over with."

When we arrived at Joseph's front door, Jack didn't bother knocking. He slid his keycard into the slot and let us both inside. "Joseph?" he called out.

Showtime.

I started chuckling and added an extra sway to my walk. "This is where the prized son lives?" I asked in a booming voice. Jack spun around and eyed me incredulously, as if I'd already fucked up the plans.

"Dad?" Joseph called from what I assumed was the bedroom. "What are you doing here?"

I replied before Jack could. "Jack always wants to clean up his son's messes." I spit on the ground just as my brother came into view. He wore a suit, and his blond hair was wet, as if he'd just gotten out of the shower.

"What is going on?"

"Hello, brother!" I added a bit of a slur to my words. "I got fired today. Apparently, you have to show up for work now? Don't they know I'm a Beauregard?" I cackled. Okay, time to tone it down.

Joseph eyed me, and the look of pleasure on his face almost made me crack. He always loved seeing me miserable and broken. "Is he drunk?" he asked Jack.

"It would appear so," Jack fumed.

Now was the moment to really sell it. "Can I go home now? It was just one tiny arrest. You can get me out of it with a wave of your magic wand, daddy-oh." I lifted a finger and pointed at them both before finding a chair to slump into.

"What happened?" Joseph asked.

Alright Gov. Beauregard. Show me how a politician lies. "I got a call at four this morning. Hamilton was stripping naked at a local bar. I had to pay off a photographer not to put it in the papers that a Beauregard was trying to coordinate a mass exodus of streakers." I started chuckling maniacally. Good job, Jack. That was very on brand for me. "I also was informed on the flight here that he lost his job this morning. I had hoped he would have sobered up a bit more by now, but..."

I ran my hand over my abs and puckered my lips. "Whatever."

"I thought he liked his job?" Joseph asked in a haughty tone.

"He did. Hamilton is always destructive, but this

is next level." Jack went to the mini fridge and found a bottle of water, tossing it at my head. I let it hit me because I had a part to play. Method acting and all of that. "For fuck's sake, Hamilton, sober up."

I reached for the bottle now lying on the floor and toppled over out of my chair. Give me the motherfucking Oscar.

"I'm assuming he and Vera broke up?" Joseph asked. "I don't get it. I mean, sure, I imagined fucking her a time or two, but I wouldn't be so pathetic about it."

Rage burned through me. He'd imagined her? What a sick fuck. Maybe forget this entire game and just beat the shit out of him now.

This felt like a test somehow. I laughed. "Vera wouldn't fuck you," I mocked. "She likes men that actually know what to do with their dicks." And then, then I let a bit of authenticity bleed to the surface. It was just a single drop, but it was enough to make my face twist in pain and my chest constrict. "Vera," I cried, hating that this brief vulnerability was on display for Jack and Joseph to see.

"Disgusting. I'm divorcing my wife and haven't shed a single tear, and he got fired from his job for some coed pussy?" Joseph asked while shaking his head. Once again, I had to force myself not to violently punch him. "I still don't understand why you brought him here," Joseph replied in a bored tone. "I have meetings and an interview with CNN later."

Jack looked at me before putting his arm around his favorite son and guiding him toward the living room. I could hear them still, but just barely.

"This could be our chance... He's heartbroken... We could put him to work..."

My brother's voice was louder. "It is easier to mold broken things, I suppose. I'm just not sure he'd even want to."

Jack replied. "Something tells me he wants any excuse to get the hell out of Greenwich. He has no job, hardly enough money to survive. He doesn't really have a choice. Bringing him in will look good, Joseph. And you can take him under your wing. Show him the ropes at our DC headquarters. I'm gearing up for reelection, Joseph. I don't have time to deal with a drunk. I need to be in Greenwich."

"I just started my new job. I don't have the time or the energy to deal with a walking, talking scandal, Father."

"He'll be fine. What better way to control him than have him work for you?" Jack asked. Oh, so now he'd caught on. My brother craved power. He couldn't resist the lure.

Joseph growled. "I heard my soon to be ex-wife is staying at your house still?"

"Just until she can get on her feet," Jack said quickly. A little too quickly.

I felt Joseph's eyes on me. Even though I was now lying on the floor, my own eyes closed as I pretended to be drunk sleeping. "Interesting. He fucks up, and you give him a job. I fuck up, and you make me get a divorce. The bruises were consensual, by the way. She liked it rough. I'm not mad about ending the marriage, even if I'm now a laughingstock, but I was having fun punishing her for the pregnancy lies."

I had to force myself not to gag. Those bruises were most definitely not consensual. If I didn't hate the bitch so much, I'd feel bad for Lilah. Too bad she was a shitty mother.

"Believe me. Working for Beauregard Industries will be plenty enough of a punishment. I'll leave him in your capable hands. I can trust you to train him? I'll make sure he has accommodations."

"I suppose I don't have much of a choice," Joseph growled back. "Whatever you want, I go along with. Right, Father?" I wished I could see the look of utter disappointment on Joseph's face. He had such angelic features that it felt sacrilegious to see Joseph so angry and twisted up with rage. "Get him off my floor, find him a proper suit, and tell him to show up on Monday ready to work."

I heard footsteps approaching. I felt his body crouch and hover over mine. I continued to pretend to sleep. Trauma was like a nightmare, reminding me of how evil he was. "You're fucking pathetic. Always needing me to clean up your messes," Joseph whispered fiercely. There was a shift in the air that was so sudden I didn't even have time to brace myself before an expensive shoe on a lethal foot was slamming into my stomach. I groaned and grunted.

I lost my fucking mind. For a brief second, I wasn't in DC on the hotel floor. I was in my childhood bedroom, hiding under my bed from Joseph. I could still feel the way his hand wrapped around my ankle and pulled me out. I could still feel the way he kicked me over and over and over in the stomach.

"Fuck," I groaned. I wanted to stand up and beat the shit out of him. Fuck this job. But the only thing that kept me writhing on the floor was the idea of revenge and creating a safer world for Vera.

"Get up, brother. We have work to do," Joseph replied before spinning on his heels and walking away. Jack didn't dare help me pull myself to my feet. He never wanted to interfere when Joseph beat the shit out of me. It was a hard kick that made my teeth rattle. I'd probably bruise.

But instead of raging, I laughed. "Want to go for a drink, Jack?"

"Shut up. Let's go," my father barked before pushing me through the door and toward the elevator. It wasn't until we were outside that I dropped the drunk facade.

"That was brilliant," Jack said. "He bought it."

"And he's going to make my life a living hell."

I waited as the limo pulled up to the front of the hotel.

Jack cleared his throat. "I'll tell you something my father told me, God rest his soul."

"Your fatherly advice is cheap, Jack," I replied.

"People can only make your life hell if you let them, Hamilton. Beat him at his own game, and you'll never have to deal with him again."

Beat him at his own game, huh?

Well, that I could do.

"*A* letter of recommendation? Are you dropping out?" Dr. Bhavsar asked while looking over the rim of her glasses at me. I felt awkward, sitting in her office. Shelves stuffed with books filled all four walls. Her oak desk was ornate and oversized. The massive furniture and leather desk chair seemed to swallow my dainty philosophy professor. Her brown skin was covered in a sheen of sweat. She had a small space heater in the corner, warming the entire space. I'd left my suitcase by the door, but Dr. Bhavsar kept staring at it.

"I'm not dropping out. Just...transferring schools."

"The semester is almost done, Miss Garner. I'm not going to waste my time or insult your intelligence by telling you why I think it's ridiculous to drop out now. Why not wait it out? Get the credit you earned, Vera."

"I'm still going to finish out the semester," I said in a rush. I completely agreed. I earned my semester of school. Jack already paid for it, and I wasn't going to put myself through the trouble of taking my classes all over again for the sake of pride. But I wouldn't be continuing my education at Greenwich University. "Thanksgiving is in two weeks and then finals. I know I've been absent lately, but—"

"I don't need excuses. I'm just surprised is all. You're one of my best students," she said with a casual wave of her hand. I couldn't help but feel proud of her comment. I'd worked my ass off this semester, despite all the...distractions.

She rolled up her cheetah-print sleeve and grabbed her cup of tea. Taking a sip, she stared at me, as if waiting for me to explain myself. How would I even begin? "Do you know who my family is?" I asked.

"The Beauregards. Influential. Powerful. Annoying as hell. Egotistical. Simple-minded. Selfish..."

I grinned. At least we were on the same page about them. "They're paying for my school and have certain expectations of me. I'd rather go somewhere more affordable than have them hold it over my head."

She clicked her nails on the desktop. "I suppose I'm just disappointed. You were one of my favorites, Vera. I was even going to suggest that you sign up for my higher-level class." Dr. Bhavsar sighed. "But I guess I can't blame you. You know my parents wanted me to be a surgeon? With my caffeine addiction? My hands shake constantly. I also have the worst gag reflex. Just the thought of cutting someone open makes me want to puke. But they persisted. In the end, I became a doctor, just not the kind they expected."

I politely laughed as she grinned at me. "Did they try guilt tripping you into going to school for medicine?"

"Something like that," she quipped, a hint of mischievousness in her tone.

"Maybe I'm too proud," I replied with a shrug. "Life is just a cycle of owing people something, you know? This school is amazing. I could easily do whatever Jack asks and just accept their generosity. It just feels wrong. And..." I paused, debating on telling Dr. Bhavsar about this. "Joseph just served my mother divorce papers. How long until they pull the plug on my education anyway? Or what if they come back and tell me I owe them for it?"

"Owing people is an evil necessity, yes? We owe landlords, taxes, parents, bosses, friends, and various bill collectors. There's a level of trust associated with going into business with someone or agreeing to a relationship in which they have all the control. Landlords can easily kick you out. Bosses can fire you. Parents can disappoint you. Humans are... tricky. And craving control over your own destiny is understandable. But it's also important to note that we can choose who we owe." I swallowed the emotions bubbling up my throat and squirmed in my seat. She looked down at the paper I'd handed her when we first got here. "So what is this for again?"

"A scholarship at a state school an hour away. I'm scrambling and might have to take a semester off to get everything in order. But the deadline is in three days, and I think I can get my essay done by then and hopefully not have any gaps in my education."

"You've had a busy morning," she murmured while looking over the requirements for the nomination. She nodded at my suitcase. "Packing, too, no doubt."

"I know your time is valuable. You're just such a notable name in your field that—"

"I'll write the recommendation. You need anything else for this scholarship? Where are you staying, Miss Garner? Have you eaten?" Her tenderness caught me off guard.

I hadn't quite figured that out yet. "I was going to figure that out after here…"

Dr. Bhavsar clicked her tongue, then stood up. "I'm done with my classes for the day. Grab your things. I'm taking you to my house."

"What? Why? I don't—"

"How would you like to owe me, Miss Garner? The way I see it, you have nowhere to stay. Four weeks left in the semester, and a lot of work to do in order to get into your new college. You can spend your time trying to survive, or you can owe me one." Her eyes twinkled, and I considered her offer. I knew Dr. Bhavsar from school. She was kind, wise, and intelligent. But it felt wrong to…

"I don't want to be a burden," I admitted. It was a common theme these days, burdening people.

"I have a spare bedroom. Get yourself a job, and I'll let you pay rent if pride is your issue. I live right by a bus station, so you can go to school easily. I also need someone to house-sit when I go to visit my parents in India over winter break. You'd be helping me, honestly."

My eyes filled with tears. I couldn't believe she was going to help me. "Seriously?" I asked.

"Don't look so shocked. I might be a snarky hard ass in the classroom, but I do care about my students."

I wiped at my eyes, the strength I'd been clinging to for the last few days fleeing my body. I slumped in my seat. Grief wrecked me. Sobs choked my body. How could this kindness from a woman I barely knew feel so much more meaningful than things given to me by my own mother?

Because it was pure.

Because there wasn't an ulterior motive.

"Vera," Dr. Bhavsar said. "Let's go to my house. I'll order some food. And you can tell me why you're crying, okay?"

I let out an exhale. "Okay."

―――――

ANIKA BHAVSAR'S HOME WAS BEAUTIFUL. CLEAN. Eclectic. Cozy. Spacious. Decorated in forest green and gold tones, with a luxurious flair that made me feel comfortable. The guest room was large and had its own balcony looking out over the street and neighboring park.

"I just can't believe you slept with your uncle. Wait—" Anika—it was still weird calling her by her first name—pulled up her phone and started typing. "I don't think I've ever seen the younger Beauregard."

We were giggling and three glasses of wine in. Sitting on the carpeted floor in her living room with my legs crossed, I let out a drunken huff. Anika was kind, graceful, and she listened to me talk for the last hour with striking attentiveness, only offering a few comments here and there. Take-out containers littered her coffee table from the food we'd eaten. It was awkward at first, transitioning from the professional authority I was used to when thinking of her and moving to something more friendly. But she assured me that when I was in her auditorium, I was nothing more than another student. If anything,

I knew I'd have to work twice as hard to ace my final essay.

"Oh," she added in a deeper voice. "He's handsome."

"You found a photo of him? That was fast."

"I just typed his name in Google. He fills out a suit, that's for sure."

My fingers ached to take her phone from her and stare at the photo. I missed Hamilton, against my better judgment; I couldn't help but feel like goodbye wasn't enough. She set her phone down and stared at me. "It sounds like you really liked him. And I can't believe Jared was a paid bodyguard. I should fail him."

She winked at me playfully and started to clean up our dinner and stack the food containers. "I already yelled at him," I replied before moving to help her. "I wanted a family, you know? In the beginning, I liked Jack. I was willing to like Joseph. I wasn't disillusioned about the wedding, but I still hoped that it would lead to something great. It's always been my mother and me. Now it's just...me."

"A lot of people have this picture-perfect idea of what it means to have a family; it makes reality a much harder pill to swallow," Anika began. "I never had any kids. Never got married. I'm not really a fan of chaining my life to someone for all eternity," she said in a soft voice, but there was a pain there. "I started the process to adopt last year, and my parents don't understand why I want to be a single mom. It's been harder than I anticipated to find a birth mom willing to work with me, because I'm in my late forties and am single, but I still have hope. I have a steady job, a calm routine, and a heart for children. I don't understand why I need a man, too."

"Do you date?" I asked, hoping I wasn't being too intrusive.

"I have in the past, but it's just not really my thing. I've had sex with both men and women, but I never really enjoyed it or felt like I needed it to survive. I want to be a mom, though. I love kids. And I truly care for women who have had to give their children up. Not everyone is strong enough to do that. I'm really sorry your mom went through such a difficult situation without the support she needed, and more so, I'm so sorry that trauma impacted your life, Vera."

I cleared my throat and took another sip of wine. "I just never got the mom experience, you know? And now I'm stuck in a relationship with what feels like a toxic best friend."

"It sounds like you set some healthy boundaries,

though," Anika pressed. "Separating yourself financially from the Beauregards, going out on your own. It isn't easy to take that leap."

"I probably couldn't have done it without Hamilton," I admitted.

"And why is that?" she asked before pouring herself another glass of merlot.

"He's been encouraging me to do that since the beginning. I always envied his ability to say fuck it and just do his own thing."

"Do you think the two of you will ever—"

Her question was cut off by my ringing phone. I looked down at the caller ID and frowned. Why was Hamilton calling me? "Speak of the devil," I murmured before looking up at Anika.

"Oh, please answer. Don't mind me. I'll just finish cleaning this up."

"I don't know if I should," I admitted.

The phone stopped ringing, and I let out a sigh of relief. "Vera?" Anika said as I stared at the screen.

"Yeah?" I sounded distracted and dejected.

"I'm going to turn on my professor hat for a moment," she said before throwing away our empty containers and walking back over to me. My phone started ringing again. "One of my favorite philosophers is Ludwig Josef Johann Wittgenstein.

Brilliant man, if not a little twisted. He said my favorite line. 'Whereof one cannot speak, thereof one must be silent.'" Anika looked down at the phone in my hand. "Wittgenstein explored the concept that there are limits to language. There are many things that can't effectively be said. Some things have to be shown, Vera."

"It's curious that he's calling me," I whispered.

"I think you should focus on the fact that he is calling you, instead of whatever words he's about to say, yeah? Didn't Hamilton want a goodbye? Why would he call if he wanted that?" I chewed on my lip. Anika had a point. "I won't judge if you answer or not. Do what's best for you. If, right now, the healthiest thing for you is to turn your phone off and eat ice cream, then I support that. If you want to talk to him and devour whatever he says to you, then that's cool too. Either way, I need to sober up so I can write this letter of recommendation for you." Anika patted me on the shoulder before excusing herself. My phone started ringing again.

"Thank you," I said. "For everything."

She waved her hand, dismissing my appreciation as if it were inconsequential. It wasn't until she was tucked back in her office on the other side of her home that I answered my phone.

Actions. I'd focus on the things not said.

"Why are you calling?" That was the first thing I'd said. No greeting.

"Where are you?" Hamilton questioned.

Did he know I wasn't at the apartment or with Jack? And what did it mean that he was looking into it?

Actions, Vera.

I decided to test him. "I'm at my apartment," I replied in a haughty tone.

Hamilton huffed. Wherever he was, it was loud. The familiar sounds of a metropolis were the background noise to his voice. Cars honking. People talking. Busses' squeaky brakes. "No. You aren't."

So he knew where I was? Why was he keeping tabs on me? "It doesn't matter where I am. We said goodbye."

Hamilton cared, despite his goodbye, he cared.

"Just tell me where the fuck you are so I can hang up the phone."

So he wanted to make sure I was safe, but didn't want to speak to me. Interesting. "I'm safe. Staying with someone for a bit while I get on my feet."

"Who?"

"I'm not obligated to share that with you, Hamilton." I stayed quiet.

"Who are you with?" he asked again.

Whereof one cannot speak, thereof one must be silent.

Whereof one cannot speak, thereof one must be silent.

Whereof one cannot speak, thereof one must be silent.

I breathed in and out, letting the noiselessness take over. Letting it consume me.

"Vera? Are you still there?"

I sat back in my seat, letting him panic for a bit longer. He cared. Hamilton pushed me away for a reason, and I was fucking going to find out why.

"Vera! Fucking talk to me. I'm just trying to make sure you're safe."

"I'm safe, Hamilton. Are you?"

My question must have caught him off guard. He exhaled, the sound full of startling exasperation.

"Well?" I pressed on.

Hamilton ended the call.

I smiled to myself.

8

HAMILTON

"Did she get the scholarship?" I questioned, holding the phone in one hand while the other adjusted the ruby red tight tie that felt like a noose around my neck.

"Yes, though the scholarship director told me she would have gotten it regardless of my intervention. She did great on her essay, and the letter of recommendation was a huge selling point. Her professors really like her," Jack replied. "They don't announce the scholarship winner until December seventh, but she'll be all set for school this spring."

"Of course she did great," I snapped, half proud and half annoyed. "She's great at fucking everything she does."

Jack chuckled. "You're welcome, though. For pulling a few strings. Even if she didn't need it. Vera is a true Beauregard. Shame the marriage didn't work out." I hated the way my father equated success to being a Beauregard. It was like he wanted to somehow take credit for Vera's hard work. My girl being great at things wasn't a shocker to me. I just wanted to make sure that she had the money she needed to start her classes in the spring. Thanksgiving was tomorrow, and she only had a couple of weeks until finals. Time was running out and her stability was the most important thing to me.

Well, perhaps the second most important. Ruining my brother was probably first.

Jack went silent, and I walked down the tarmac to the Beauregard private jet. Jack wanted to do a family Thanksgiving at his house, and I was required to attend. Joseph went there a few days early to meet with his lawyer about the divorce, and was staying at a nearby hotel, which meant I didn't have to fly or stay with the insufferable bastard.

My uncomfortable Gucci shoes clicked along the pavement as I walked, briefcase in hand. It cost a lot of money to look like I had a lot of money. I had a part to play, after all. Crazy how quickly I acclimated to my new role in the company. I fucking hated it. I fucking hated everything about it.

"Your first few days on the job seem to be going well. Have you learned anything?"

"I learned that you waste a fuck ton of money on pointless things," I replied.

Jack laughed. "Like what?"

"You just purchased an office space with an arcade for your employees," I huffed with a scoff.

"Employee satisfaction is good for business, Hamilton."

"Want to make your employees happy, Jack? Use that money to extend maternity and paternity leave and offer better health insurance." Despite benefiting from it my entire life, I hated capitalism. "You have incredible wealth, and some of your employees are living just above the poverty line, Jack. You're a politician, sworn to serve the public, and yet you cash in on crazy profits without redistributing the wealth to your loyal workers."

I marched up the steps, waiting for him to respond. "You seem to have put a lot of thought into this," he noted.

"I've had a lot of time on my hands. Joseph got me an office and told me to sit there and just research the different corporations you own. It's boring as fuck. He doesn't want me doing anything. I've learned a lot though. You have a tech company in San Francisco that's data mining and selling pretty fucking intrusive information to advertising agencies. A logging company in Arkansas that's ruining the ecosystem and barely complying with sustainability laws. An oil subsidiary off the gulf—one that I used to work for—that is cutting corners on a few health and safety standards. It's a massive oil spill just waiting to happen, by the way."

"I thought you were working to figure out what Joseph was up to," Jack replied calmly.

"You wanted me to audit Beauregard Industries, and I am."

"Just don't lose sight of your purpose. You aren't there to make massive changes to our operations, Hamilton. My team is plenty capable of making sure we comply with federal and state laws. I want you researching Joseph and finding the laundered money."

"It feels like you dropped me off at a burning building, Jack. You have more ethical problems than just your psychotic son. It's pretty shitty that you're barely following laws that you helped sign off on."

"If you want to discuss your concerns, I'm all ears. But you've only been on the job a handful of days. Let's chat when you realize how many people rely on our companies to survive. Let's chat when you have a better grasp of the laws." I was ten steps ahead of him. I'd already sent all the information to Saint to research. "I was thinking," Jack added.

"Happy to know you're capable of producing thoughts, Jack," I growled into the phone before nodding at the pilot and making my way to one of the plush leather chairs.

"Maybe we should invite Vera to Thanksgiving? Her mother is staying with me, still. I know Lilah would love to see her daughter—"

"Absolutely not. The whole point of this is to keep her away. Why on earth would I invite her to an awkward Thanksgiving with her mother, Joseph, and me?"

Jack clicked his tongue. "I'm trying to keep Lilah happy so she feels comfortable opening up to me.

Inviting Vera would do just that. Not to mention, I figured you'd like to see her instead of getting all your information secondhand. And besides, I thought you knew. Joseph isn't coming. He had some business in San Francisco to attend to."

I was fuming. "Don't you think that's important information for me to know? What kind of business in San Francisco, Jack?"

"I don't know. You're the one that should be following his schedule, Hamilton."

"We're supposed to be a team, Jack. I need to know when Joseph has random business trips!"

Jack let out a huff of air. I rolled my eyes. "Perhaps you're distracted by Vera? Maybe if you didn't spend all your time calling me to ask what she's up to, you'd be able to focus on your job—your real job, not just this research you're conducting on things unrelated to the task at hand."

It took everything I had not to hang up on my father. "Vera isn't a distraction, Jack," I gritted. "She's the only reason I'm even helping you right now. Make that suggestion again and I'll quit on the spot. Keep your fucking opinions about her to yourself, or we'll have a problem, got it?"

Jack chuckled. "You're obsessed with the girl."

"That sounds an awful lot like an opinion I didn't

ask for. It's nothing you don't already know. My obsession is partly why I agreed to help you in the first place, Jack. Drop the conversation. And I better not see her at Thanksgiving. Pretty soon, Vera won't need me anymore, and I won't have to keep tabs on her."

"Too bad love doesn't work like that," Jack mused in a soft voice.

"What the fuck is that supposed to mean?"

"You're always going to find things she needs, Hamilton."

"You're the last person to offer advice on love and needs."

Jack liked to pretend that his marriage was unspoiled, and not sensuous panic. One of my favorite things to do was remind him that he was a failure. It was almost blasphemous to compare his sham of a marriage to what I shared with Vera. He wouldn't know what was real if it died in front of him in a bathroom. Jack continued, "—and the faster we figure out what Joseph is up to, the sooner you can be done stalking her."

"I'm not stalking her," I gritted.

"Whatever you say."

I had a million things I wanted to say to my father. I still didn't understand why it was so important I bring down Joseph. I wanted to ask him if he lived his whole life feeling this way. Privileged. Powerful. No wonder my brother became a nut case. Just having a private jet at my disposal gave my ego a complex.

"How is her mother?" I asked. "Has she revealed anything incriminating about Joseph?"

Jack cleared his throat. "She's fine. Still staying here, as you know. Missing Vera very much. I guess we both expected her to apologize by now. Lilah and I both decided that it was probably better that she wait to move out after the divorce is finalized."

"Right," I drawled. "Are you fucking her?" It had only been a week, but I put nothing past my father or Lilah.

Jack audibly gasped over the phone. "Of course not. Don't be so crude." Yeah. Dad was totally fucking her. But I didn't care. Vera was out of her toxic mother's life, and Jack was close to getting useful information from Lilah. I didn't give two fucks how he acquired it, as long as he did. That woman had to know something about Joseph.

"Tell me about San Francisco?" I demanded. The door to the jet had been shut, and we were about to take off.

"Our tech company is out there—the one that

most definitely does not data mine, as you so eloquently put it," Jack argued, his voice low. "We also work with a small manufacturing company out there. We buy goods from them regularly."

"Does Joseph normally go there?" I pressed while pulling out my laptop and sending Saint an email with this news. We had made plans to meet up while I was in town. Thank fuck these jets had Wi-Fi. A guy could get used to traveling like this.

"Lilah did mention he traveled a lot. She claims it was an affair," Jack droned on as I pulled up the flight logs for the family fleet of jets. My brother had been traveling quite a bit lately. Joseph wasn't in the habit of going out of his way for pussy. Flying across the country on the regular to get laid wasn't exactly his MO.

But for money? Power? My brother would do anything for that.

"I'll let you know if I find anything," I grunted. Joseph was still suspicious of Jack and me, which made navigating this entire situation more perilous. I thought Joseph would make my life hell and enjoy slapping me across the face with his massive ego every chance he got. But no, he just tucked me into a quiet corner and pretended I didn't exist. It wasn't his usual play.

"Is he still giving you trouble?" Jack asked.

"He's pretending I don't exist. I think you need to encourage him to actually include me. Maybe he didn't think I'd actually stay?"

"Or maybe he's suspicious," Jack replied.

"Just keep learning, keep acting interested. If Joseph puts you in the corner, get up and insert yourself into meetings and what not. It's still new. I'm...I'm proud of you for actually trying, Hamilton."

My heart constricted, and I wanted to break the phone currently in my hand. I hated the way I preened at his compliment. I was ashamed to be happy and was disgusted with myself. I was a Beauregard, and I was good at it.

Jack Beauregard was proud of me. Me. His bastard son and ultimate disappointment.

"I've got to go. I've got some reports to comb through. I finally got those profit and loss statements you sent over, and it takes me twice as long to understand the numbers as anyone else. Bye." I had to remind him that I was shit and he was supposed to be displeased that I didn't go to college or all the other things he expected of me. We had a game to play, after all.

I didn't wait for Jack to respond and hung up the

phone. How did we go from barely talking to having multiple calls a day? I felt like I'd sold my soul.

"We're departing, Mr. Beauregard," the flight attendant said with a smile before serving me a glass of champagne.

"Thanks," I replied rather gruffly as she bent over, giving me a healthy view of her tits.

Nothing, it did nothing for me. The flight attendant was cute. She had blonde hair, plush lips. An ass I could eat for dinner. Her sultry smile should have gone straight to my cock, but I felt zilch at the idea of fucking her a mile in the air. I didn't want her. I didn't want anyone but Vera Garner.

"I'm busy," I said when she lingered. Our family shared this plane, so maybe she was used to getting dicked by my brother and was hoping to fuck the hotter Beauregard.

"Of course," she said with a smile before disappearing.

Once in the sky, I ignored my briefcase—yeah, a fucking briefcase—and started scrolling through the photos on my phone. Vera filled my screen.

She was a warrior. She didn't need my help, not really. She got her philosophy professor to write a bomb ass letter of recommendation for her job and applied for aid at the state school she mostly qualified for with grades and merit alone. Vera moved out of the apartment Joseph and Jack got her the day after Lilah announced the divorce. She found a place to live—I'd originally thought she'd moved in with Jared, but was pleased to find out that she was staying with her philosophy professor.

Maybe I was a fucking stalker. I didn't care. Vera deserved better than what she got, and I respected her need for independence. I didn't want her tied to the Beauregards any more than I was.

I was staring at another photo of Vera when my phone started ringing. Jess. Fuck, I missed my best friend. I felt like shit for blocking her from my life. She didn't understand what I was doing, but it was necessary to keep her safe. The facts were starting to add up, and it wasn't looking good. If Joseph was involved in what I thought he was, then the retaliation would be brutal. He wouldn't let go of his empire without a fight, and I wasn't going down until he had a knife in his back and an empty wallet.

I let the phone ring and go to voicemail. Jess was probably cussing me out right about now.

Too bad. I was in this for the long haul. Save Vera. Protect Jess. End Joseph's nasty reign over our family.

Easy enough.

Jess: Are you coming home for Thanksgiving? We need to talk.

I stared at the message. Yeah. For the first time in my fucking life, I'd be sitting at my father's table for Thanksgiving.

Hamilton: No.

9

VERA

*W*hen Jack Beauregard invited me to Thanksgiving dinner on my mother's behalf, my first instinct was to laugh uncontrollably and tell Jack to get fucked.

But I couldn't do that. Because I wanted to see how my mother was doing. And because I had a feeling Hamilton would be there. The red dress," Anika said. She was sitting on the end of my bed, flipping through the papers we turned in before

Thanksgiving break. I'd gotten an eighty-six on mine, proof that she was going extra hard on me now that I was living with her.

"It's a little sensual, no?" I asked before pinching my bottom lip with my teeth.

"That's the point," Anika replied with a sigh.

I looked at my reflection and frowned. The tight dress hit just above my knee and exposed all of my back. The heart-shaped neckline accentuated my breasts, and my long hair covered my exposed shoulders. I felt beautiful in the dress—one of the few things I took from my previous apartment. I'd fallen in love with it the moment Jack had his personal stylist deliver a completely new wardrobe.

"I feel exposed."

"Sometimes, that's the best way to feel," Anika said, "But come on, I've got a black leather jacket that will make you look badass."

I grinned as she got off the bed and disappeared for a moment. I slipped on some kitten heels and reapplied my lip gloss. By the time she returned, I was almost ready to face them.

"Here," she offered before tossing it at me.

I ran my hand along the rough leather. It was beautiful.

"Thank you. I love it."

Anika looked proud as I put it on. "So, let's discuss healthy boundaries before you go. Tell me your mantra again."

"I am not responsible for how other people act," I recited. Anika was on board for me going—if anything, just to ease my plaguing mind about Hamilton and what he was up to.

"Now, tell me you're safe."

"I'm safe," I repeated while grabbing my purse.

"Tell me you can leave at any time you wish."

"I can leave anytime I wish."

Anika was researching a study about the effects of vocalizing your intentions, and somehow, I'd become her guinea pig. I didn't mind though; it was nice to have someone care. She was so healthy, so mature and fun. We had a good relationship. I was worried about awkwardness because she's my professor, but I still felt that same level of respect in the classroom. She wasn't my friend, per se. She was more like a close mentor who cared about my mental health.

"I'll be attending Friendsgiving with some of my colleagues, but I'm just a phone call away, okay? I'm really proud of you for doing this. I think it speaks volumes about your maturity to be able to confront her again. Sometimes people don't realize that you have to put in the work. It's not just enough to tell someone off, then cut them out of your life. Sometimes you have to fight that daily fight, you know? You have to work on yourself still."

I nodded. "Thanks."

"And you always have a place here, so fuck them if you don't like how they treat you. There's nothing hanging over your head anymore. You're in charge of your own destiny, Vera Garner."

————

BEING AT JACK BEAUREGARD'S HOME FELT WRONG. I had a store-bought pie in my hand and my purse slung over my shoulder. There wasn't a bone in my body that wanted to go inside. Every step toward the front door felt like giving up.

"I can leave any time that I want to," I whispered to myself before balancing my pie in one hand and knocking on the door.

I cleared my throat and tried to paste a smile on my face. I was here for answers and closure, nothing more.

The door swung open, and my mother flashed me a brief, fake, extraordinary smile before twisting her expression into confused disappointment.

"What are you doing here?" she asked in a snippy hiss.

"Jack invited me to Thanksgiving. He said this was your idea?"

"It most certainly was not," Mom replied. "Jack and I were going to have an intimate dinner together. Alone. Hamilton said he wasn't feeling well this morning and..."

I looked my mother up and down. Short dress. Cleavage for days. Fake eyelashes with a longer wingspan than most birds. Bright red lipstick the color of my dress.

"Intimate dinner, huh?" I asked. Seriously? She hadn't talked to me in a couple of weeks, probably didn't even know where I was living, and the first words out of her mouth were to leave? Typical. So fucking typical.

"Please tell me you aren't hooking up with your soon to be ex-husband's father, Mom. Please. You're so much better than that."

"Considering you fucked your uncle, I don't think you have much room to talk. Hell, pretty soon he'll be your stepbrother, if I have any say in things."

"Jack will never marry you. He cares way too much about his image for that. You thought that hooking up with Hamilton was bad? Just wait until the press gets ahold of this."

Mom looked around and curled her lip before pushing me further outside and joining me on the patio. Quietly, she shut the front door and crossed her arms over her chest. "I'm working on something. I really don't need you fucking this up for me. I know how much of a scandal this could be if this got out, which is why I'm making a point to keep our new relationship under wraps. I can't do that if you're here crashing our Thanksgiving dinner, Vera."

"You're going to blackmail him," I replied in shock. "You're going to threaten to go to the press if he doesn't pay you off, aren't you?" I asked. The realization hit me almost instantly. She was going to seduce and use Jack. Part of me didn't really care, perhaps my former grandfather deserved the injustice after everything he'd done.

It wasn't the victim who had me concerned, it was my mother. Who had she become? Why was she using her body like a weapon? "You're unbelievable," I scoffed. "Seriously, Mom. Why? Why would you do this? Why not walk away?"

Mom looked around once more before lowering her voice. "Joseph owes me, Vera. And thanks to the ironclad prenup they had me sign, I'm not going to get a dime unless I do this."

A slight breeze slapped against my cheek, stirring up my curled hair. "What do you mean Joseph owes you?"

"Let's just say I helped him with something. I was supposed to get cash, but he backed out on our deal." Why did she sound so cocky?

I didn't like how she'd adopted the Beauregard way of speaking in riddles. "What do you mean you helped him with something? Something illegal?"

Mom pressed her lips together. She looked like a fortress, determined not to let a single secret past her teeth. "I'm not telling you. I'm not sure I can trust you anymore, Vera. Please, just leave." The pleading tone startled me.

"No, I think she should stay, Lilah," Hamilton's deep voice interrupted. I spun around and met his teasing stare. He wore khaki pants and a button up shirt with a navy blue blazer that accentuated his muscles perfectly. His hair was awkwardly swept to the side, as if he were trying to look like he was going to the local country club.

Seeing him was devastating. It was like looking at a stranger but also gazing into the eyes of a soul I knew intimately. It hurt to see him, but it excited me too. I couldn't get my body to process how to respond to the pain and utter delight.

"Hamilton, I thought you weren't feeling well."

He walked up the front steps while practically ignoring me. "I felt better. Shall we go inside?" He held out his arm to my mother, and she reluctantly accepted it. The two of them went through the front door without a word, and I stayed behind for a moment to go over my mantras.

I could leave any time I wanted.

I was safe.

I had a place to live.

I was not tied to the Beauregards any longer. I could do this on my own.

I turned, half ready to leave. Hamilton didn't even look at me. It was like I didn't exist. What did that even mean? Could I handle a day of sitting at the same table as the man that both broke me and built me up?

"Are you coming, Vera?" Jack asked. I hadn't even seen him approach. I waited at the threshold, my breathing turning panicked. Opening my mouth, I tried to form words, but nothing came.

"Vera? Are you alright?" Jack asked the question as if he already knew the answer. I shouldn't have come back here.

"I..." I breathed harder; my vision tunneled. I hadn't expected to panic at the sight of Hamilton. I was supposed to be here to figure out what the fuck was going on.

"Vera? Why don't you sit down, you look like you're about to pass out."

"Here," I choked out before thrusting the pie into Jack's arms. "I have to go."

It took all the strength I had to force those words out. I felt stupid. Childish. Who was I to take on this pain and get to the root of it? I forced my stiff legs to turn my body around and walk back down the drive. A bus? I needed a bus.

"Lilah? Come quick. I think Vera is going to pass out."

I moved faster, not wanting my mother to pretend to be the hero, pretend to care about my well-being, pretend to give a shit about anyone but herself.

Harsher breathing. My eyes swam with tears. I could barely move.

Strong arms wrapped around my body, and I slumped in relief, instantly recognizing who it was that held me. "Whoa, Petal. Are you okay?"

No. I wasn't okay. I was losing my fucking mind. And for what? A man who didn't want me back? A mother who was more preoccupied with getting money?

I thought I was strong enough to handle this, but I fucking wasn't. I felt stupid. "Is she okay?" my mother called. "Maybe you should take her home, yeah?"

Hamilton picked me up and cradled me to his chest, as if I were a broken doll or a baby. "I'm going to take her home," he called over his shoulder, the tone mirroring disgust. "Happy Thanksgiving." He then murmured under his breath, "Selfish bitch."

It was wrong—so wrong—but I pressed my face to his chest and breathed him in. I let him carry me to a BMW I didn't recognize. It had temporary license plates and every upgrade you could imagine.

I focused on my breathing.

I inhaled. Exhaled.

The rising panic continued to consume me. It felt like everything was crashing around me, and I couldn't process it. How had my life become so complicated? Would it ever end?

I sat in the front seat and stared at Hamilton as he circled the hood and got into the driver's side. "What happened, Petal?"

I breathed in and out. "I'm safe," I whispered. "I feel stupid. Seeing you and talking to my mom shouldn't fuck me up in the head as much as it does."

"Why'd you show up?" Hearing the question shared so bluntly shamed me some. I honestly didn't know how to respond. Why was I here? Was it for closure? Did I show up because I craved the drama? Did I have something to prove to my mother? Maybe I just wanted to feel strong for a little bit and show off how much my mother's decisions didn't affect me anymore.

Or maybe I just wanted to see Hamilton again. He was an addiction I couldn't quit.

"I had some questions. Needed some closure. Plus, I've never had a real Thanksgiving before and thought, what the hell."

Hamilton twisted in his seat to look at me. "You've never had Thanksgiving?"

"When I was little, Mom started a tradition of McDonald's for Thanksgiving. She couldn't afford a turkey, and our first apartment only had a hot plate and a microwave. As we got older, she just kind of kept up with it. Depressing, right?"

Hamilton cursed under his breath and started driving away from the house. "What closure do you need?"

"You said goodbye. But then you called me. I'm

trying to wrap my head around what you're doing with Jack. I saw in the papers that you're working for Beauregard Industries again. Why? And why do I care? You can't be happy there...but it doesn't affect me. A smarter woman would move on with her life and just..."

I was rambling.

"Here's the thing," I quickly added. "I feel like you're working with your father because of me. Tell me I'm wrong, Hamilton. And you know what sucks? I can't even tell if I hate it or am thrilled by the idea of you being willing to work with Jack."

Hamilton gripped the steering wheel tighter, his face a mask of indifference. "Thrilled? Does it get you hot to see me like this, dressed up in a suit and driving a car worth more than what I used to make in a year?"

I rolled my eyes. "I'm thrilled that you care about me, Hamilton. Because despite the way you treat me, and leave me, and hurt me, I fucking love the idea of you loving me back."

"I don't get how you can just forgive people. When I walked up the drive and saw you talking to your mother, it just infuriated me. You were done with her, Vera. You told her off and walked out like

—" His tone was cold, his charcoal eyes black and pinned to the road in anger.

"How did you know about that?" I asked.

"It's not important," he quickly snapped. "What's important is that you just stood there having a calm conversation like nothing had ever happened."

"Forgive me for trying. Is that what this is about? You want to be punished, Hamilton? You're working for your father because you think you deserve to be miserable? You're pushing me away because you don't want us to be happy?"

Hamilton pulled over the car, the deserted winding road hugged by a tunnel of barren trees. Dead leaves littered the ground. Hamilton reached over and unbuckled my seatbelt. "What are you doing?" I asked.

"Making you happy, Petal."

10

I was a certifiable dick. I honestly deserved to have my ass kicked. I didn't deserve Vera. I'd fucked her and walked out the last time we were together. "You can't fix everything with sex, Hamilton," she snapped at me, her fiery eyes wild with challenge. I knew that look on her face. Lust. Need. She fucking wanted me, despite it all.

"Sex fixes plenty of things, Petal," I whispered before leaning over the console to trail my lips over her exposed neck. Goose bumps broke out over her creamy skin. My eyes zeroed in on the heaving rise and fall of her chest. And then—she fucking slapped me away, like I was a dog trying to eat her steak dinner.

"Back the fuck off, Hamilton Beauregard. You hurt me."

I swallowed and looked at her. The bite in her tone went straight to my dick, which made me feel like even more of an asshole than I already was. It was such a pussy move to push her away. "You hurt me too, you know," I countered.

Her brows raised. "Is that really how you want to play it?" she asked, challenging me even more. Fuck yes, Vera. Call me on my shit.

"I'm not playing anything. Why'd you agree to that arrangement with Jack, huh?"

"Because at the time, I didn't feel like I had any other options," Vera quickly replied. "I made a snap decision with the information I had at the time. My mother had just shown up beat to hell, and the man I was falling for betrayed me in the worst possible way. The only thing I had was school, and Jack was holding that over my head. I made a choice. And then I changed my mind," she said while crossing her arms over her chest. The move pushed her tits up, and I had to rip my eyes from the beautiful sight of her cleavage.

"You could have talked to me—"

"No, I couldn't. You didn't even try to reach out after shit went down. Honestly, if it weren't for Jack, I would have never spoken to you again, Hamilton."

Yeah, no, fuck that. Not talking to Vera ever again wasn't really an option anymore. I physically couldn't keep away from her. So much for pushing her away for her own good.

I wasn't going to let Vera walk out of my life forever. I was too far gone, too stuck in her orbit. Loving Vera was an inevitable consequence of knowing her. It was impossible to stay away. I just needed a little more time. I wanted to build a life for us that was safe and free of my bullshit with Joseph and my resentment of Jack.

"Are you saying I should be thankful that Jack basically manipulated you into reaching out to me?"

"I guess that depends on whether or not you give a shit about me, Hamilton? Why are you working with Jack? Why are you driving me home? Why are you ignoring me one minute, then trying to get in my pants the next? Why are you—"

I cut her off with a kiss, because I couldn't stand not having the taste of her on my tongue. Because I wanted to swallow her words and make things better. The seatbelt strained against my body. The center console cut into my stomach as I swept my tongue over hers. She tasted like mint gum.

Moans filled the car. She was driving me insane. Her hands pressed against my chest, but I didn't budge, though. "Petal," I groaned, the needy tone so desperate I knew she'd figure me out.

She pressed against me again. "You haven't even apologized yet," Vera choked out between kisses.

"I'm sorry, Petal." I sounded desperate. I needed her forgiveness like I needed air, the beautiful irony was claiming her mercy was as easy as opening up my lungs and fucking breathing. I'd been too damn stubborn.

She ripped away from me on a choked sob and opened the car door. It took me two seconds to realize she was running away from me. "I can leave anytime I want to!" she yelled the moment I got out of the car and chased after her. The deserted highway was the only witness to our emotional moment.

"Vera, get back in the car. You can't just walk home!" I threw my arms up and dropped them at my side as she stomped ahead of me, her heels sinking into the wet earth with every step.

"I can leave anytime I want, Hamilton," she repeated. I chased after her and nearly collided with her when she spun around to face me. "What the fuck kind of apology was that, Hamilton?" she asked, her voice an emotional screech. She lifted both hands and shoved at my chest. "You want to fuck again? Is that it? Am I just someone you can use again?"

"Petal..."

"Don't call me that!" she screamed. I watched helplessly as she looked up at the sky. "Why'd you have to go and be like everyone else, Hamilton? Why'd you have to hurt me like that?"

"I'm trying to protect you!" I roared. That was the whole point of this shit, to not be like everyone else in her life. To not demand her forgiveness and abuse it. But here we were, and I wasn't any better than her mother, or Jack, or Joseph. I was just another person making Vera Garner cry, and I hated myself for it.

Vera froze on the spot. "Who are you trying to protect me from, Hamilton?" she whispered. "Jack? Joseph?"

I looked at her and let out a sigh. Lifting up my hand, I stroked her cheek for a gentle moment before responding. "From me, Petal. From the inevitable shit storm that's about to rain down on us."

She shook her head as more tears fell. "I risked it all for you," she whispered. "I would have given you anything. And you know what's worse than you hurting me, Hamilton? It's the fact that I still care about you! I still want you to be happy. I still want to pick apart your mind and figure out what hurts you —what heals you. Does that make me weak? Does it make you happy to know that I'm so fucking torn up about all of this?"

"I was trying to avoid this, Petal," I whispered. "You want the truth?" I don't know why I was telling her this now. I just couldn't stop the honesty pouring out of my mouth.

She gave me an incredulous look. "You're kidding, right?"

I grabbed Vera's wrist and pulled her to the tree line. I didn't want any cars driving by to see what we were about to do. "I fucking love you, Vera. I can't stop thinking about you. I know where you're staying right now, because the moment I wake up, I have Jack give me an update on your life. I know you got the scholarship for Connecticut State University, because I had Jack call and make sure you were awarded it." She started breathing heavy, a storm brewing in her brown eyes. I pushed her against the trunk of a tree and continued speaking. "The day after you found out about Saint, I drank myself stupid. The next morning, Jess kicked my ass and demanded I come beg for your forgiveness. You want to know why?"

Vera swallowed as I pressed my body against hers. "Why?" she whispered.

"Because she knew you were the best fucking thing to ever happen to me." I kissed her neck. I ran my hands up her sides. I breathed her in. "And that I was a complete dumbass for not being honest with you."

"So why didn't you try?"

"It's dumb."

She grabbed the belt loops in my pants and tugged at me. I wasn't sure I could get any closer than I already was. "Tell me." Her nostrils flared with barely contained anger.

"I knew I was just going to fuck it up again," I admitted defeatedly. Saying my fears to Vera was harder than I anticipated.

"You stupid, broken man," she whispered back before slamming her lips to mine. The wind kicked up her hair as she curled her leg around my body. The trunk of the tree hid us from the road where an eighteen-wheeler zoomed by. "Stop pushing me away."

I inhaled sharply and pressed my forehead to hers. "I thought sex couldn't fix everything." I was teasing her, but she didn't smile. We both knew that I was just trying to lighten the mood.

"I'm not fucking you out here, Hamilton," Vera said in a soft, steely voice. "You've been in control of us from the beginning. I've been helpless to stop this since the moment I met you. But you know what I just realized?"

She pushed me away and dropped to her knees. Fuck. The sight of her in the dying grass with her cheeks rosy and her eyes sparkling with mischievousness. I almost came right then and there. "Wh-what are you…"

She unbuttoned my pants and pulled out my hard cock. I'd never been so ready for a woman. "You're not in control anymore, Hamilton. If I want to get hurt by you, it's my choice. If I want to forgive you, that's my choice, too. If I want to suck you off out here, I'm not doing it because I'm a fucking martyr who likes to suffer. I'm doing it because I want your cock in my mouth. I'm doing it because I am my own person now."

"Vera—" Her lips pressed against the head of my

dick, and she placed a soft kiss on my hot flesh. I twitched and jerked from the featherlight touch. "Fuck."

"Don't try to save me, Hamilton. I don't need a hero. I just need you."

She wrapped her glossy lips around me and slipped me fully into her mouth. I tossed my head back, shocked at how good it felt, her lips pressing together to make it hot, wet, and tight. When I bumped the back of her throat, she gagged a little bit. Drool collected in the corner of her mouth. She looked up at me with angry eyes and wild hair. I gathered her chestnut locks in my fist on top of her head and guided her movements. Faster. Nastier. Harder. Pleasure like nothing I'd ever experienced wholly consumed me.

Every little moan had me shaking with need. I felt myself building, building, building.

She pulled away and gasped for air before going back to sucking the fucking soul out of my body with her talented little mouth. My muscles contracted. I moaned. A car drove by. The leaves under my feet shifted and crunched. A beam of light burst through the clouds. Heat. More wind picked up. Pleasure. A beetle climbed up the tree trunk. Nirvana. The woods witnessed our naughty declaration, and my queen? Fuck, she kneeled before me, taking all the power and control for herself.

And then she stopped.

I nearly toppled over. I was so close. So fucking close. "Why'd you stop, Petal?"

She grinned and wiped her lips with the pad of her thumb. "I can leave any time I want to," she replied. What the fuck was with this phrase, and why would she want to stop now? "We could be good, Hamilton." She licked my shaft with her warm tongue.

"We are good, Petal."

I leaned forward, bumping my cock against her lips in silent protest. I wasn't going to beg for her mouth, but I sure as fuck would encourage her to keep doing what she was doing.

"You don't get to end this because you're afraid I'll get hurt, Hamilton," she whispered before rising to her feet.

No. No, no, no.

"Petal—"

She grabbed my chin and squeezed. "I'm the one in control. I choose who is worth fighting for. I don't get on my knees for martyrs and cowards." I breathed in. My dick was out. My pride was shot to hell. I wanted to tell her everything. I wanted to make this right.

But then my phone started ringing. What the fuck now?

She wrapped her delicate fingers around my cock and tucked me back in my pants. Slowly, ever so slowly, she inched the zipper back up and fastened my button. I was so close to the edge that I felt like I was going to explode. "Aren't you going to answer that?" she asked before licking her lips.

"FUCK!" I screamed. I'd created a monster.

I grabbed my cell out of my pocket and answered it with a growl. "What?"

Jack immediately replied, "Joseph is meeting with one of our distributors. I need you on a plane to San Francisco."

"What? Right now?"

"Now. I've already got the jet ready. Drop off Vera and get your ass to the airport."

I stared at Vera. We absolutely had some unfinished business, but this could be the moment we'd been waiting for. Maybe I could figure out what Joseph is up to way ahead of schedule. "Fine. I'll go."

I hung up the phone. Vera spun around and trotted over to the car, as if she didn't just have my dick in her mouth. As if I hadn't spilled my fucking guts to her.

"Vera?" I called.

She looked over her shoulder and smiled at me. "Take me home, Hamilton."

What the actual fuck?

I shook my head, then jogged to the car. Once inside, we both sat there for a moment. I didn't know what to say. "I have to go on a trip," I whispered.

"Okay," Vera replied, her tone soft and genuine. I tried to sense if she was upset with things, but she had a grin on her face.

"I feel bad about just leaving after what just happened," I continued.

"Why? I'm the one that gave you blue balls." She clicked her seatbelt and grinned. "You're going to go off and do whatever you're doing with Jack. But you're going to be thinking of me." She turned to face me and leaned in. "You're going to ache, Hamilton. You're going to have a hard cock, and nothing will ease it. Not your hand. Not memories of me. Not another woman. Me."

Fuck, was it possible to get even more turned on than I already was? I inched closer. I craved her lips again. "Petal," I whispered.

"Go do whatever it is you need to do, Hamilton.

Now that the roles are reversed, I'm going to be for you what you were for me." My girl, she smiled, obviously proud of herself.

I combed through the haze of lust and pulled back. "What?"

"You taught me how to stop being a martyr and take control of my life. Now I'm going to do the same for you, Hamilton."

11

HAMILTON

"If you don't get your hand off my cock right now, I'll dump my drink on you," I growled low in the woman's ear. Hailey...Heidi, Heaven, Hannah. That was her name. Hannah something. She was pretty enough, and if I weren't hung up on the girl that haunted me—mind body and soul—my dick might have liked the attention. But my dumbass didn't want Heidi, Heaven or Hannah.

I wanted Vera. Vera Garner.

"Your brother said..." she began, confused at my dismissal.

"My brother was misinformed."

She stared at me in confusion for a moment before dropping her mouth open and saying, "Ohhhh. You're gay. Dad in politics? I get it. Your secret is safe with me." This girl was so full of herself that the only plausible reason in her mind for not wanting her was being gay? Arrogant little thing. "We already got some photos together, so my publicist will be pleased. Mind if I go dance?" She was already getting up and scanning the club for her next victim.

Fuck this place.

She honestly wasn't worth the effort. "Have a great night, Hailey."

"It's Hannah," she corrected me, brow arched in annoyance with her hands placed on her petite waist.

What the fuck ever. Just leave me alone.

My phone buzzed, and a text from Vera came through.

Vera: Thinking of you.

Yeah, I was thinking of you too, Petal. I couldn't stop thinking about the way she wrapped her lips around my cock. I couldn't stop obsessing over her intense behavior and the way she took charge of the situation. Our dynamic changed in an instant. I couldn't quite make sense of it, but I liked her newfound confidence. She was cocky, almost. Aside from Jess, I'd never known someone to have so much blind faith in me.

I quickly typed up my response.

Hamilton: Stop texting me. I told you to leave me alone.

We both knew my refusal was half-hearted at best. Why was I pushing her away again? It had almost become a game between us, a test. Her response was swift.

Vera: How is San Francisco?

How the fuck did she know I was here? Another text pinged through.

Vera: I like the suit. The tabloids don't do you justice.

What tabloids? I tossed my phone on the table top in front of me with a sigh. Coming here was a huge mistake. The second I got off the plane, Joseph was waiting for me on the tarmac, a smug grin on his face. It was as if he expected me to follow him here. I expected him to shrug it off and come up with some bullshit excuse, but no, he dragged me to some fucking nightclub.

I was about to order something other than this shitty champagne when my asshole brother and his cocaine-nosed date plopped down opposite me at the table we reserved in the VIP section. The club was opulent, modern, loud, and smelled like pot. Being here was a waste of time. I didn't think it was physically possible to convince my brother I wasn't up to something, but I had to try. None of this was adding up. The laundering seemed way too sophisticated. No matter what paper trail Saint and I followed, I couldn't pin down the source. Jack had an entire team working undercover and none of us were any closer to figuring this out than before.

"At least pretend to be having fun, Hamilton. It cost me twenty grand to get this table, and that champagne you're ignoring is more than most people make in a year," Joseph said, his nose tipped to the sky as his date rubbed his upper thigh. Asshole.

"I am having fun," I lied. "Lots of fun. So much fun I can't stand it." My dry tone was impossible to misunderstand. I didn't bother lying to Joseph because if I wanted him to trust me, I had to be believable. Suddenly changing my entire personality would raise too many red flags.

Joseph was wearing a suit, the collar of his shirt stained red from his date's lipstick. There was something satisfying about the way he swayed in his seat. Despite being wary of me, he was letting his guard down with the alcohol. He'd also disappeared in the bathroom for a long while, which made me wonder if he was sneaking off to the bathroom to do drugs.

It would be easy, to lunge across this table and stab him in the eye with my bottle of expensive champagne. I imagined how it would feel to snap his neck in front of all these people, spray his fucking blood all over the expensive carpet. "Did you hear a word I just said?" Joseph asked. The girl was sucking on his neck now.

"Nope. I'm too distracted by the girl trying to suck your face off."

Joseph smiled and gently pushed her away. "Pretty thing, isn't she? Want to try her?" The woman snapped up in her seat, and her brow dipped.

I frowned. "I'm not a fan of secondhand pussy, brother. We've never really been a family that had to settle for hand-me-downs, yeah?" I asked before taking a drink of the overpriced champagne. The bubbles brightened on my tongue, and I swallowed them down with bitter triumph.

"You got my secondhand mother, did you not? She was worn out by the time you were born. Like those sneakers you used to be obsessed with that had holes in the soles." Joseph nodded at one of the cocktail waitresses, who then pulled the red privacy curtain around our table, hiding us from view from everyone else.

I was livid, furious with his careless words. But I had to play the long game. "Mom was depressed," I replied as Joseph eased down the zipper on his pants. His date licked her lips triumphantly.

"Suck my cock," Joseph demanded, ignoring me. I shifted in my seat, prepared to leave, when Joseph held up his hand to stop me. "Stay. I've been wanting to chat with you."

My brow arched. "You want me to watch you get your cock sucked?" I countered. "Disgusting even for you."

"Don't make it sound so vulgar, Hamilton. It'll just alleviate my stress for when you inevitably piss me off. You know what happens when you piss me off, don't you?" Joseph grabbed the back of his date's head and forced her down so hard that she gagged and slurped. Thudding music pounded around us.

Anxiety flowed through me like a crashing wave, but the only outward expression of my nervousness was the way I silently tapped my foot. "Suck me harder," he commanded her while folding his hands behind his head and leaning back in his seat.

"What do you want to talk about," I gritted. This was so fucked up.

"Why are you really here, Hamilton? Why are you working with Dad? The old you would have punched me in the face and marched out of here. But look at you, sitting there and watching me get off. Like a child playing dress up. I bet I could kick your ass and you'd just let it happen."

His date bounced, bobbed, and moaned on his lap. I felt bile travel up my throat. It was taking everything I had not to puke right here in the VIP booth. I had to keep my cool. I had to fucking navigate Joseph's insanity, dig through his power plays with a silver spoon. "Is this about Vera? You had such a unique connection with my stepdaughter, didn't you?"

"You know I dated Vera," I said. He wanted us to end our relationship.

Joseph let out a pleased grunt that made my stomach clench in disgust. "Vera's a pretty girl. Can't blame you. Was she good?" He stopped talking to moan. The timing of his question and the subsequent sound of pleasure had me raging. No. He wasn't allowed to think of my girl like that. Fucking perverted son of a bitch.

"That's none of your fucking business."

"You still love her. Cute," Joseph said before grabbing his date's head and thrusting up into her mouth. "I like knowing who's important to you." He started pumping in and out while suffocating the poor girl. I averted my eyes until I heard him come, feeling weak and disgusted with myself as she whimpered. Fucking sick fuck. "What does dating Vera have to do with working for our father?" he asked. I looked up at him as he adjusted his clothes. The girl was still wiping her face when he tapped her on the cheek and nodded at the curtain. "Leave."

She didn't even argue.

Joseph's ominous words were intended to make me angry, but I knew without a shadow of a doubt that he'd have to go through me to hurt a hair on Vera's head. She was safely away from his psychopath ass, and I might not have been able to defend myself all those years ago, but I'd murder him with my bare hands without a second thought.

Once his date was gone, I answered my brother. "Vera wanted nothing to do with the Beauregards after you served her mother those fucking divorce papers. She felt betrayed by our family and broke up with me immediately." It wasn't too far from the truth. She'd despise the man I was now. Nothing about this life appealed to her. We couldn't be more different now if we tried.

"Okay. Whatever," he replied with a wave of his hand. "I'm still trying to work out what you're up to. Despite your performance with Dad, I'm not convinced. You always were such a pathetic little martyr, but it would take an act of God to get you working for the family business. Come on, be honest with me," Joseph said while leaning forward threateningly.

I let out a huff of hot air. "I don't know, I normally wouldn't give two shits about this company, you, or Jack. I'm not sure if I ever will. But I needed a change of pace. I wasn't too thrilled when Vera and I ended things."

Joseph shrugged. "Fair enough, you lying motherfucker. Those Garner women sure do fuck a man up. That bitch, Lilah, can rot in hell. She has me feeling particularly vindictive."

There was at least one thing Joseph and I could agree on. "How are you handling the divorce?" I asked.

He scoffed. "Did you not just see the hot piece of ass sucking down my cum just now? I thought the best day of my life was when I found out Lilah wasn't having my baby, but it turns out, the best day was actually when Dad asked me to dump her ass. I thought he'd care about his precious political image. You know how testy he gets with bastards running around." Joseph swept his eyes up and down my body. "But since Lilah was lying, I didn't have to do a damn thing. That article saved my life, Hamilton. Didn't your half brother write it? Do send him my thanks. Funny how things work out."

I clenched my jaw. Fine. If we were going to be honest about this shit, so be it. Pretending and lying wasn't going to work with Joseph. Maybe it would be better to keep him on his toes. "You're right. You don't need to know why I'm suddenly interested in Beauregard Industries," I began while standing up and fixing my suit jacket. "You just need to know that I'm not going anywhere."

"That's an adorable threat. I'm trembling from fear, little brother."

"It's not a threat. I'm simply claiming my birthright."

Joseph scoffed. "The birthright of a bastard?

Please. You barely deserved your job on the oil rig. You're a nobody."

"I'm a Beauregard," I growled.

He chuckled. "Saying something over and over doesn't magically make it true."

I clenched my fist and surged forward, grabbing the lapels of Joseph's jacket and pulling him up. "Shut the fuck up, you pathetic motherfucker."

He tipped his head back and laughed. "Hit me, Hamilton. Maybe it'll make you feel like a man."

I jerked him around. "Is that why you hit me all those times, huh?" I asked. "Did it make you feel strong? Did it make you feel good to break my arm?"

Joseph smiled. "I suppose I would have felt something if I cared at all about you. But you were nothing, Hamilton. Just a toy to toss around." I shoved him back, and he fell against the velvet VIP couch. His entire body slumped, and I watched as he started helplessly laughing. His arms folded at his middle, and his pores leaked rancid, alcohol-soaked sweat. Once his laughter subsided, he spoke. "You can put on a suit and ride around in our jet. You can even sit in meetings like you know what you're doing. But you'll never be good enough. You'll never be a Beauregard. Because a Beauregard would have punched me just now."

12

$\mathcal{I}$ stared at my phone, forcing myself to adopt the natural confidence that Hamilton personified.

Vera: I'm thinking about you again. Are you aching, Hamilton?

He didn't respond, but he saw the message. I wasn't giving up, and I wasn't going to hate myself for fighting for what I wanted, either.

Standing outside of Jess's apartment building,

my acidic chest bubbled with nerves. I thought I'd have enough time to brave up and confront her during my forty-five minute bus ride, but I was still just as nervous now as I was two days ago when Hamilton left for San Francisco and I decided that I needed to talk to Jess.

If anyone knew what was going on with Hamilton, it was his best friend. I just hoped she'd talk to me. It would take an army of fiercely loyal people to pull him out of whatever mess he was involved in. I made up my mind to approach the situation the same way he pursued me: with unwavering determination.

I marched up the steps to the top floor with my head held high. Once I made it to her doorstep, I hovered my fist over the door and paused.

What if this was a mistake?

What if Jess didn't want to work with me?

The door opened before I could knock. Jess arched her brow and glared at me. "How long are you going to stand outside our door, Vera?" she asked, forgoing the usual greeting.

"However long it takes," I admitted before letting out a huff of air. "Just trying to figure out what I'm going to say to you."

"Who says I want to even hear what you have to

say?" she snapped back before crossing her arms over her chest. Jess looked worn down. She was wearing thick glasses that barely hid the exhaustion in her eyes. Her sweatpants hung low on her frame, and the oversized T-shirt looked like one of Hamilton's.

I tilted my chin up, despite the growing sympathy filling me up at the sight of her. Gone was the submissive Vera, the one that let people walk all over her. I wasn't in the wrong here. I had every right to talk to Jess about Hamilton.

She shifted from one foot to the other, waiting for me to speak.

"You hurt me," I began.

"So what?" she countered on a snarl.

"You knew about Saint."

"I did," she replied.

"That's pretty shitty, Jess. I get that you have loyalty to Hamilton. I suppose at the end of the day, you don't owe me anything. But I'm not going to let you be mean to me after the shit you pulled. I'm here because I care about Hamilton, and so do you."

Her eyes widened, the dark depths of her gaze filled with surprise. A couple of seconds passed, and she remembered that she was supposed to be short with me. "You don't care about him! You're the reason he pushed me away!"

"Who the hell are you to tell me who I care about?" I straightened my shoulders. "He's shutting you out, isn't he?"

"How do you know that?" she asked, her voice full of anguish.

"Call it a hunch."

The resolve and pride in Jess's shoulders slumped. Tears suddenly filled her eyes, and she reached out, grabbing me for a fierce hug. She sobbed as she held me, and I stood there dumbfounded for a moment before patting her back. "It's okay," I said, mostly because I didn't know what else to say.

She pulled away and wrapped her hand around my wrist before yanking me inside her quaint apartment. I took a brief moment to look around, taking in the small, closed off floor plan, the tiny loveseat placed in front of a flat screen, and various musical instruments placed all around as if they were art pieces. "What's going on?" I asked.

"He's not answering any of my calls. I went out with him, the night you guys broke up. He was stupid and got trashed. Almost went home with some milf, too."

176

My heart stung, but I kept listening, trying my damnedest to keep a straight face. "Okay? Then what happened?" Even though I had a pretty good idea of what had happened next, I wanted to hear Jess's version of events.

"The next morning, he just wasn't himself. I tried to get him to get you flowers and go apologize, but he kept saying he didn't want to be another person that abused your forgiveness. He talked about your mom. I think he was afraid he'd end up being just another person that let you down."

Jess stopped talking to grab a tissue and blow her nose. I absorbed her words and sat down on the loveseat. "Then what?" I asked.

"Then he asked me to leave. I was prepared for him to go on this massive bender. I thought he'd do his usual—stay busy until he passed out. But he didn't do anything, Vera. He just sat in his living room for like four days. I stopped by, but he didn't want to see me. I've never seen him like that. And then all of a sudden, he's working for Jack? What the fuck? He doesn't want anything to do with those people. This isn't like him. He never ignores my calls. I've been saved by Hamilton my entire life, and the one time he really needs me, I failed him—"

"You did not fail him," I promised. "He's up to something."

My phone started ringing. "Speak of the devil," I whispered.

"That's him? Let me answer!" Jess nearly fell over herself trying to answer the phone, but I jerked it away from her.

"I don't want him to know we're together just yet," I hissed. She didn't look amused, but I didn't care.

"Hey there, handsome. How's San Francisco?"

"Why do you keep texting me?" he asked, his voice warm and alert.

I looked at Jess. "Oh, darling, I miss you too. What are you wearing?" I grinned playfully at his best friend, who looked at me like I had two heads.

"What the fuck are you doing?" she mouthed. I ignored her.

"Vera. I told you already. I'm not—"

I cut him off. "Right. You're not going to date me. You don't want me. Blah, blah, blah. So should we have Christmas at your new place in DC? Or should we meet at Jack's house since the two of you are so close now?"

It shouldn't feel this good to beat Hamilton at his own game, but I couldn't help it.

"How long are you going to do this? We're done, Vera."

"We're done when I say we're done," I replied, albeit a bit manically. "If you want me to slow down on the stalker tendencies, you know what you have to do."

"And what is that?" Hamilton asked, sounding amused and not at all as angry as he was supposed to be.

"Tell me the truth. Tell me what you and Jack are up to. I can help you."

I wasn't expecting the seriousness in Hamilton's response.

"You want the truth, Vera? I'd give anything in the world for a thousand more goodbyes from you. I'd love to meet up. I'd love to sit here and listen to you talk for the rest of my life. I want to be with you. I want to hold you. I want to do all the stupid things couples do. I want to take you to dinner at my mother's favorite restaurant. I want to tell you everything. And maybe one day, I will. But right now, I'm not going to risk you."

My heart practically sored. Despite the pain his words brought on, there was hope there too. "Is this how it felt?" I asked.

"How what felt?"

"Watching me bend over backward for a mother that didn't give two shits about me," I answered. I bit my lip, but he didn't comment on my observation. "Let me come to you. We can figure this out."

"Don't."

"But you just said—"

"Haven't you learned by now, Petal? We don't get what we want. I'm going to block your number now. Please don't call me again. I don't want to be cruel to you. But I will. I'll break you so fucking beautifully if it means keeping you out of this. Goodbye."

Hamilton hung up the phone. I looked at Jess. "Well?" she asked.

His words might have been meant to deter me, but it just emboldened me more. I wasn't going to roll over and let anyone else control my life anymore, even Hamilton. "He's in something bad. We have to get him out," I whispered. "I don't know what's going on, but the man I just spoke to sounded defeated."

"What are we going to do?"

"We're going to go talk to him, of course." An idea came to me suddenly. I quickly scrolled through my contacts and clicked Jared's name.

"Vera?" he answered. "What a nice surprise."

"You owe me, Jared."

Even though I couldn't see the party-hard playboy, I imagined him pouting on the other end of the line. "You're so predictably boring, Vera. Our fight is so last month."

I rolled my eyes. "Are there any events coming up with the Beauregards that you can get me into? Since the divorce, it looks like I've lost my invitation to every upper class social event coming up."

"Oh, is there trouble in paradise? Do you want to ambush your uncle? How scandalous. We should have a threesome."

"Absolutely not. Can you get me in or not?"

Jared sighed. "The Beauregards are hosting their annual winter charity ball. I have it on good authority that your lover boy will be there now that he's all up in the Beauregard business. He looks good in a suit, yeah? You can be my date if you'd like? I'll buy you a slutty dress, and we can make him mad with jealousy."

Beggars couldn't be choosers. "That sounds great," I answered.

"Wait. Really?" Jared asked.

"Really," I replied dryly.

"Well, shit. You must be desperate to see him. And I get to pick your outfit? I'm really picky about my dates. I want them to stand out, you know?"

"As long as I'm not naked."

"And can I kiss you in front of him?" Jared asked mischievously.

"No."

He laughed. "Deal's off then. I'll only take you if you let me kiss you. I really wanna rub salt in the wound, you know?"

"You're impossible, you know that?"

"Is that a yes?"

"Fine. But I'm not responsible for what Hamilton does afterward." I was absolutely not going to kiss him, but Jared didn't need to know that. "And I want you to bring my friend, Jess, too."

"Sorry, love. Only got one ticket. They're like ten grand a pop, you know."

I nearly choked on my shock. "Fine," I argued. "Where even is it?"

"It's in DC," he replied easily. "I'll get us a nice, romantic hotel room."

I scowled. There was no way I'd be sleeping with Jared, but I didn't really have many other options. "Okay, but you should probably get a suite so there's enough room for Jess. She'll be my ride to DC."

Jess crossed her arms over her chest and nodded at me. "What? We can just fly. I told you I'm rich again, right? Mom rearranged some of the charity funds since I'm basically a charity case. Shh. I probably shouldn't be telling you that. No cap."

"I'm not using your mother's charity fund for a first class flight to DC, Jared. I'll meet you there."

"Fine. Your loss."

"Goodbye," I sang, eager to get off the phone before he gave me any more ultimatums or tried to add sex to the deal. Jared really was a pig.

"Bye, sweetheart."

Once I was off the phone, I looked at Jess. "We're going to get Hamilton."

She watched me for a moment before grinning. "I knew I liked you."

13

The Beauregard winter charity ball was a spectacle without substance. Expensive designer shoes clicked against the floors. Long evening gowns trailed behind beautiful women. Chandeliers made of pure crystal hung overhead. Strobes illuminated the walls, and popular music played through the speakers. A supposedly famous DJ was setting up for a set. It had a polished nightclub vibe that I knew would give me a roaring headache by the end of the night. The universe practically kneels at the feet of these privileged patrons. At ten grand a plate, the people who bought tickets to this event weren't motivated by donating to the Beauregard Foundation—a charity that had raised millions for underfunded schools and provided significant tax write-offs for a billionaire or two. They were paying for the extravagance. They were paying to be seen, to rub elbows with other members of the elite.

The annual Beauregard charity auction was created to raise funds for schools in underfunded districts. It was a great cause, but the original intention got lost in the luxury of it all. My father could just write a check and save himself the hassle. When I stumbled across the cost that went into planning an event like this, I practically choked on my tongue. I had no desire to be here. Now that I was stepping up to work with Joseph, everyone wanted a piece of me. I was no longer the forgotten bastard son.

I used to love attending shit like this. By the end of the night, I'd be getting some heiress off with my fingers in the middle of the dance floor just to embarrass my father and cause him some problems with the press. But making a scene and skipping it wasn't an option. Ever since San Francisco, Joseph had become more secretive. Going to California was a wash. He didn't meet with anyone. He just spent the weekend getting drunk, getting high, and getting off with whatever hot piece of ass he could find. Jack thought that maybe he was having a bit of a mid-life crisis thanks to the divorce, but I wasn't convinced. He knew I was coming, and he switched up.

My phone pinged and I checked my messages. Vera hadn't sent a text all day, and it made me sick. Ever since Thanksgiving, she'd been persistently checking in on me. I hated how much I looked forward to her naughty requests and sentimental updates. I rarely replied, but her determination connected us and made me feel at peace. It also gave me hope that at the end of this, we could be together. I just had to sever my ties with the Beauregards first.

Saint: We need to meet tomorrow. Jack is sloppy. I don't trust him.

I quickly answered with the time and place before pocketing my cell and scanning the crowd for my brother. Jack certainly was sloppy. I had a lot of thoughts on what he really had up his sleeve, but I'd play my part and bide my time all the same.

"You look nice, son," Jack said. I didn't bother turning to greet him.

"Your personal stylist is pretty good at their job," I replied casually before taking a glass of champagne off the tray of a passing waiter. "Did you bring your new girlfriend? Or are you keeping her hidden at your house?"

From the corner of my eye, I saw Jack's cheeks turn red. He tipped his chin up. "I have no idea what you're talking about."

I took a sip. "I'm not judging. Just because I think she's a narcissistic psychopath doesn't mean you can't get your dick wet. I'm all for pissing off Joseph."

Jack straightened his bow tie. "Lilah is staying with me until she can get on her feet—"

"I once read that if you repeat something over and over again, it helps you to believe it."

Jack lowered his voice and hissed at me. "She's telling me things about Joseph."

I turned to face him. "Is she, though? Joseph somehow knew I was going to San Francisco. He met me at the airport, actually." I downed the bubbly champagne and burped obnoxiously while Jack frowned. "Where is my brother? I heard Gary Herbert is going to be here. Joseph's secretary mentioned that he calls Gary a lot. He has a vacation home in San Francisco, too."

Jack swallowed. "Gary? Gary Herbert is a major investor."

"I'm just being thorough, Jack. Isn't that what you wanted?"

"Of course I do. That's the whole point of this. I just don't want you pissing off the wrong people, Hamilton." Jack hadn't noticed Joseph walking up, but I did.

"Who are we pissing off?" Joseph asked before clapping his hand on my shoulder harshly. I pressed my lips together, imagining all the curses I wanted to hurl at him. He was a little too bright today. Wired and energetic. He was absolutely on drugs.

"Me," I lied. "You seem to be in a good mood," I noted, changing the subject.

"Well, there's a lot to be happy about, little brother," he replied before wrapping his arm around me and dropping a bleached smile for a photographer. "Profits are booming. Our shares have never been higher. Ever since getting my cushy new job on the President's cabinet, practically everyone wants to do business with a Beauregard. It's..." Joseph paused to slowly inhale through his nose. "Invigorating."

"Don't get cocky, Joseph," Jack scolded him.

"Come on, Jack. Let loose. It's good to celebrate on occasion," I replied. "I was looking at the balance sheet for one of our tech companies, and the cash flow seems almost...unbelievable."

Joseph cocked his head to the side. Shit. Maybe I'd said too much. "Don't bother yourself with an accountant's job, brother. Just enjoy the power."

Jack cursed. I pressed on. I didn't want the fucking power. I wanted to catch Joseph and be done with this. "I'm ready to learn more. Do you have any meetings coming up? Maybe I could go with—"

"Is that why you followed me to San Francisco?" Joseph asked, a mischievous twinkle in his bright blue eyes. "I didn't think you'd be so dedicated to your new job." Joseph looked at Jack, his eyes narrow. "You must be so proud of your son. Stepping up. Following me across the country to learn more about the business. It's almost suspicious." Joseph waved at someone walking by before continuing. "If you have questions, all you had to do was ask Jack. He used to go with me all the time to meet a few of our business partners."

"Like Gary Herbert?" I asked.

Joseph twitched slightly before clearing his throat. "Gary is a good friend of mine. Tell me, with all your snooping, have you found anything useful, Hamilton? Or is this another game you somehow roped our father into?"

This time, it was Jack's turn to look uncomfortable. He shifted on the balls of his feet.

"I don't know what you're talking about," I lied.

"Sure, you don't," Joseph replied in a low voice before straightening his spine and looking around the room before continuing. "Oh, look. Vera is here. Jack, I'd assumed you'd bring my ex-wife since you're fucking her now, but I didn't realize you'd bring her daughter, too." My father looked like he was about to shit himself.

"What?" Jack sputtered before frantically scanning the room. I couldn't bring myself to look. I was terrified that I would, in fact, see Vera at this party. I took a second to hope that Joseph was just fucking with us.

My brother let out a low whistle. "Wow. She's a looker, huh? I should have gone for the newer model. Easier to groom into what I need, don't you think?"

I snapped my head to stare at Joseph. "What did you just say?" My tone was a feral growl.

Instead of answering me, Joseph nodded toward the other side of the room, his face full of malice as I followed his gaze. There, wearing a champagne dress that sparkled under the flashing lights and molded to her healthy curves, stood Vera Garner. The girl I loved. The girl I was trying to save. And next to her? Was fucking Jared.

"Oh man, I guess she moved on," Joseph whispered in my ear. "We should go say hello. It's the polite thing to do after all. And I'm so thrilled to see that she reconciled with Jared. They make a cute couple, yes? But where is Lilah, Father? No need to be ashamed. Once you get over the initial scandal of slumming it with a teen mom, it really can be quite fun." Joseph's grin grew wider, and he tipped his head back to laugh.

"Excuse me," Jack grunted before pushing past us and toward the exit. Fucking coward.

"I think I'll go say hello," Joseph said, not bothered by his father's embarrassment or outburst. I reached out and grabbed his arm, stopping him from walking over to Vera. Joseph lazily looked down at my hard grip and shrugged me off. "I know it's your brand to cause scenes at important Beauregard events, but don't forget that you have much more to lose now than you did a few months ago, Hamilton," he threatened before fixing the sleeve of his tux and sauntering off toward Vera and Jared.

His threat infuriated me. But he was right, I did have a fucking shit ton more to lose. What the fuck was she doing here? And why was she with Jared of all people? I thought we understood one another. I thought she'd give me more time to figure my shit out. Why couldn't she listen? Why couldn't she just move on with her fucking life? I couldn't make up my own damn mind.

I started walking toward them, following after my deranged brother. My eyes locked on her beautiful body as I fast walked through the crowd to get to them. It was like time fucking slowed. The light hit her bare shoulders perfectly. Her long lashes framed her sparkling brown eyes dripping with honey hues. Jared leaned closer to whisper something to her, and she stiffened, obviously uncomfortable. I didn't like how she reacted to him. I also didn't like how close his lips hovered over the ridge of her ear. A cocktail waitress walked in front of me, blocking my path.

Jared placed his hand at the small of Vera's back and pulled her flush against him. My heart pounded. He licked his lips. She stared at him with a look I couldn't place. Apprehension? Amusement?

Was she not here for me after all? Had she moved on?

Jared leaned closer and did the stupidest fucking thing he could have possibly done. The motherfucking cunt slammed his lips to hers. She placed her hand on his chest and pressed. She looked limp, weak from the kiss. My entire soul crashed and burned right there on the spot. The only reason I got my legs to work was because I wanted to rip them apart and remind Vera who she belonged to before tearing out his throat.

When Jared pulled away, he looked far too satisfied for my tastes. Vera's gloss clung to his lips, and her stunned expression twisted into disgust. Thank fuck. If she would have had that adorable dazed look on her face, I probably would have had to murder someone. She used the back of her hand to wipe her mouth and winced.

Joseph laughed just as I caught up to him, and the sound drew both Jared's and Vera's gazes. Her mouth dropped open when she saw Joseph, and I noticed the way she shifted closer to Jared, as if the asshole could actually protect her. Fuck that. He couldn't do shit. I closed the remaining distance between us just as he greeted them. "I'm surprised to see you here, Vera. How are you, darling?" Joseph noticed a photographer taking photos and licked his lips.

"I've never been better," Vera answered while looking up at him. Another camera clicked.

Joseph wiped at his nose and breathed in on a sharp hiss. "We're still technically family. The ink hasn't quite dried on the divorce papers. Why don't you come give daddy a hug?" I felt stuck. I couldn't risk it all and cause a scene, but I wanted to keep my brother as far away from Vera as possible. He wrapped his hand around her wrist and pulled her in for a hug. His arms caged around her tightly, and she looked like she wanted to recoil from him, but his strong grip wouldn't let her.

"Joseph," I began. "Enough."

My brother pulled back and grabbed her chin. "I'm just giving the girl a proper greeting." Jared, being the fucking coward he was, took a step back. "How's your mother doing? Last I saw her, she was pretty beaten up about the divorce." Fucking dick choice of words, motherfucker. Vera caught on to his meaning, too, and stumbled a bit. "You understand though, don't you? We just weren't a good fit. I once read that sometimes children of divorce think it's their fault. I hope you don't feel that way, Vera. If you ever need to talk about your feelings, my door is always open. We can even have a sleepover if you'd like." Joseph tilted his head to the side before looking at Jared. "It seems you've moved on from my brother."

Jared cleared his throat. This was so fucking awkward. I just wanted to take her away from here. "Good to see you again, Mr. Beauregard. You too, Hamilton." Vera is his goddamn date. Shouldn't he at least attempt to protect her dignity? Joseph offering to have a fucking sleepover made my blood boil, but Jared was sticking out his hand for Joseph to shake.

I intercepted and ended up squeezing Jared's hand so hard I heard his knuckle pop.

"Great to see you, Jared. Now why don't you get the fuck out of my sight?"

Jared's brows lifted in amusement.

"Oh, but I was having so much fun," he countered. Vera let out an exasperated breath as he wrapped his arm around her and pulled her close to him.

"Let go," I growled.

Joseph laughed and flicked at his nose again. "Oh, don't be so bitter, Hamilton. We can all be adults about this."

"Shut up," I snapped at Joseph. "Don't you have

something you should be doing? This is your event after all."

"Our event, brother. Ours. And besides, this is significantly more fun than this stuffy party. Kiss her again, Jared. Maybe Hamilton will go postal and punch you in the jaw. Are you man enough, Hamilton?"

I took a steadying breath.

Vera must have grown some confidence, because she finally spoke up.

"Hamilton doesn't have to punch people to feel powerful, Joseph. In my experience, only people with little dicks and a superiority complex feel the need to express themselves with violence."

The humor drained from Joseph's face. Jared was pressing his lips into a thin line, forcing his face into a stoic expression, though I imagined he wanted to let out a boyish giggle at her words.

"Sometimes a situation requires a firm hand, Vera."

"What situation requires a man to hit his wife?" she pressed in a lower voice while taking a step closer. I could tell that she was emboldened by the crowd. He couldn't do anything here, but that didn't mean he wouldn't retaliate later.

"I'd be thrilled to enlighten you in a private

setting, Vera. Just say when," Joseph replied, matching her intense stare with a cruel one of his own.

No. I wouldn't stand here and let him threaten her. "Why hide, Joseph? If you try to enlighten anyone about anything, I'll chop your dick off and toss it in the punch bowl over there. I'm not as needlessly violent as the rest of the men in our family, but I won't stand here and let you threaten Vera, either."

Jared shifted from one foot to the other. "This is a little too intense for my tastes. You're all harshing my high. Vera? Would you like to go back to our hotel room? These charity events are so stuffy."

Our hotel room? Like hell she was going back with him. What the fuck? Was she staying with him? No. Nope. No. Absolutely not.

"I was actually enjoying this little family reunion. I'll meet up with you later, okay?" she said with a confident smile before turning her attention back to Joseph.

Jared looked at her, then back at me. "Are you sure?"

Without blinking, she held Joseph's stare while replying to her fucking date. "Positive." Jared didn't wait to be told twice. With an awkward nod, he scampered off like a poodle.

I started speaking the second he was gone. "Vera, why don't we—"

"Why is Hamilton working for you, Joseph? Are you blackmailing him? Are you threatening him?"

Joseph laughed. "I'm afraid I have no idea why my brother has a sudden interest in the family business."

Vera crossed her arms over her chest. "For some reason, I don't believe you."

I needed to end this conversation now. Where the fuck was Jack? He was supposed to keep Vera far away from all of this shit. That was half of our deal.

Joseph took a step closer, and I followed suit. I was about to position myself between them like a human shield. "I'm not sure I like what you're insinuating, Vera."

"I'm not sure I like you at all, Joseph," she snapped back. Long gone was the timid woman that hid from confrontation.

"Your mother was stubborn, too. Defiant. It was easy to break her." That was a fucking low blow. I wanted to open my mouth and fight back, but I was stuck. I didn't plan for this.

"You like breaking things, don't you? Does it

make you feel like more of a man?"

Joseph smiled and lowered his voice. "I'd love to show you just how much of a man I am, Vera."

"Enough," I cracked. Both of them turned to look at me. "Joseph, don't you have donors to impress?" I asked.

Around us, the entire party seemed oblivious to the estranged conversation we were having. I suppose to any onlookers, we looked like a happy little puzzle, each piece making up a fractured family.

"I suppose I do. Not nearly as fun as making Vera squirm, though." Joseph adjusted his bow tie and twisted to look at me. "You ought to know, Hamilton. Be careful with Garner women. They like to trap you with their filth."

"You're unbelievable," Vera said, her mouth curled in disgust.

"Careful. Maybe I'll decide to take your mother back." That was a legitimate threat. Joseph had no honor or morals. He'd string Lilah along just to piss off Vera.

"Vera, let's go." I grabbed her arm and pulled her over to me, thanking God that she didn't pull away from my touch.

"If you find out why my brother is working with

my father, please let me know. I'm still trying to figure out what he's up to," Joseph called at our backs before spinning around to talk to someone else.

"Where are you taking me?" Vera asked as I pulled her through the large open doors and toward the valet.

"Home."

She wiggled out of my grasp and cursed. "I'm not going home. I came all this way to talk to you and figure out what the fuck is going on. Hamilton. I'm not letting you—"

"We're going to my home, Vera." I looked around and noticed a couple women whispering and staring at us. "I want to go somewhere we can talk without people hearing, okay?"

Vera squinted at me, obviously not trusting my words. "You're going to actually talk to me?"

"Yes," I answered hastily. Her eyes sparkled with tears. Shit. I couldn't handle when she cried. I just wanted to fix this.

"Why?" she asked.

Fuck it. I pulled her close and seared my lips to hers. It was the most satisfying kiss of my life. She felt warm in my arms. Like home. Like everything I needed and more. She moaned and deepened the kiss, wrapping her arms around my neck and pressing her body to mine. If kissing Vera was a job, I'd happily clock hours for the rest of my goddamn life. But we had shit to talk about and things to work through and Joseph to take care of.

I ended the kiss and stared at her. So fucking what if anyone saw? I couldn't hide my feelings for this girl even if I tried. Joseph already knew. Jack wasn't upholding his end of the deal. Why should I have to suffer?

"Because it's physically impossible for me to stay away from you, Vera," I replied. "And because you make it impossible to protect you when you keep showing up. If I can't push you away, then I'm going to have you at my side." Her expression was dazed as I pulled her toward the line of limos waiting to take their drunk owners home. We were about to get in the limo when I remembered something. I halted with the door open and looked at my girl. "Text Jared and let him know that it's my house you'll be at. It's my bed you'll be warming tonight, and if he ever touches you again, then I'll pin him down and take a lighter to his lips."

She swallowed, but she didn't look scared. If anything, my threat turned her on.

"Will do," she whispered.

14

VERA

*H*amilton's rental house in DC was strikingly different from his home in Connecticut. It was nothing like what I expected. Cold. Everything about it was cold. Marble floors. Sleek lines. Stiff, modern furniture that didn't look inviting or even comfortable. The open concept plan was spacious but overwhelming all the same. I could see how a person would feel lonely here. The entire house just swallowed you whole.

Masculine art covered the walls and looked curated by someone trying to make a statement, not by someone who actually knew Hamilton. And the kitchen? It was state of the art but looked barely used. I wondered if I would find leftover takeout in his fridge instead of ingredients for the meals he loved to cook.

"I'm going to get Little Mama. I've had to kennel her because she likes to chew up the baseboards here when I'm gone. I think she's trying to punish me for leaving."

I resisted the urge to tell him that I shared the same feelings as he turned and walked away. I wrapped my arms around myself and steadied my nervous breathing. A door opened, and I recognized the familiar sounds of Little Mama's whine.

Soon, she shot down the hallway like a cannon headed straight for me. I didn't even have time to hike up my dress and crouch to her level before the happy dog was tackling me to the ground. Her sweet excitement almost brought tears to my eyes as I scratched behind her ears and she messed up my makeup with her slobbery tongue. "I missed you too, sweetie."

After a few more minutes of excited cuddles,

Hamilton pulled her off me and let her outside in the back patio that had a strip of grass.

I was still sitting on the tile floor and looking around when Hamilton returned. This wasn't a home. This was a glorified hotel. "I miss your townhouse," I managed to whisper while dragging my index finger along the floor. Not a single speck of dirt. It was clinical, almost.

"I miss a lot of things," he replied before walking closer and holding out his hand to help me up. The moment our fingers touched, a thrill shot down my spine. I'd never felt such a heavy sense of promise and anticipation.

Tension hung thick in the air, and he asked me if I wanted a drink. I shook my head and wrapped my arms around myself. "This is awkward," I admitted.

Hamilton grabbed a water bottle from his massive fridge and took a sip. I eyed the movement of his Adam's apple with lusty apprehension. "This doesn't have to be awkward," Hamilton replied before wiping his mouth with the back of his hand.

Pursuing Hamilton and knocking down all his walls had been so exhausting. Up until now, I had forced myself to be strong and brave. I made the effort because I knew he was worth it. I knew that we'd figure it all out in the end.

But now that we were in the silent privacy of everything that happened, I didn't know where to start.

"I hate that you're working with Joseph. This house, this place, these events, this job—it isn't you." I looked at his tux, the handsome cut so severe and sharp. It was like wearing a costume.

Hamilton circled his kitchen island and grabbed both my hands. As he led me to the living room, I watched the dim lights cast shadows along his face. Slowly, we sat down on his couch, and he pulled my legs over his lap. "I didn't get a chance to tell you earlier. But you look beautiful," he whispered.

I looked down at the dress and grimaced. "I almost had to wear lingerie," I replied with a sigh.

I watched his fingers work the heels Jared bought me off my throbbing feet. "And why would you have had to wear that?" he asked in an even tone despite the vein throbbing in his neck.

"I had to convince Jared to bring me to the event. He wanted to pick out my outfit and charged a kiss."

"That dumbass motherfucking cunt whore dinky dick—"

"Whoa," I interrupted with a harsh laugh. "Calm down." Hamilton's jealousy shouldn't excite me as much as it did.

"So he bought this dress?" he asked while rubbing my foot.

"Yes," I replied.

"Take it off." Goose bumps broke out on my skin. "We can talk, but I won't be able to think straight with you wearing a gown another man bought you. Please?"

"And what if I don't?" I asked.

"Then I'll tear it from your body with my teeth, Petal."

Another shiver rocked through me like a shockwave. Promises, promises.

The only thing I wanted more than sex with Hamilton was a conversation with him. "Fine," I replied. It took me a moment to stand up and ease the zipper at my side down. Hamilton watched me with heated eyes, his mouth parted slightly, his hands rubbing up and down the tops of his thighs. The soft fabric fell on the floor, and he gulped. My nude, strapless bra pushed my breasts up, and the lace thong I wore was practically see-through.

"Fuck, Petal," he rasped.

"I'm cold," I replied with a shiver.

He opened his arms, and I crawled into his lap, letting Hamilton warm me up. It felt so perfect to be here with him. We still needed to work through shit, but I was here. I was with him. I was his.

He grabbed a throw blanket and carefully tucked it over us before speaking. "When I first started working with Saint, the only thing that motivated me was revenge," Hamilton admitted. "We had a common enemy, and I needed his help. I thought there was power in the press. I wanted the world to know how shitty Joseph was, because my own father didn't believe me."

Hamilton started massaging my back. "I know why you worked with Saint," I replied. Even if it hurt to be used, I still understood Hamilton's motivations for doing it.

"Working with Saint was actually really fun. I felt like I had a brother for once. A real brother. I've been conditioned to fear family, but for the first time in my life, I was comfortable with someone. It's really hard to reconcile the fact that my second chance at having a brother was your living, breathing nightmare."

My breathing deepened. Hamilton closed his eyes, and I wanted nothing more than to dive into his brain and get a front row seat to what was going through his beautiful mind. "Keep going," I encouraged him.

"Then I met you. You were like this precious gift wrapped in thorns. Mine, but also not mine. Too precious for words. I didn't want to jeopardize you but was afraid to lose my new brotherhood with Saint."

I wanted Hamilton to have people in his life that he could count on. Aside from Jess, he seemed to have a very lonely childhood. "I understand," I whispered. "But what about now? You pushed me away, and then we..."

"I was just trying to keep you safe. I am finishing what I started. I'm working here to bring Joseph down. It was too good of an opportunity to pass up. I don't want you to think that I love revenge more than I l-love you, Petal. It's more like, I can't even begin to fully love until I get rid of this cloud hanging over my head."

I reached for his cheek and ran the back of my hand down his stubble affectionately. "You don't have to do this alone. If you would have just been honest with me, we could have talked about all of this and been in it together."

Hamilton leaned into my touch. "I already dragged you into my revenge scheme and hurt you. I'm working with Saint again—this time behind the scenes. I can't trust my father, either. but I'm working with him to figure out what illegal activities Joseph is up to."

"Okay. Let's do this together, then."

Hamilton twisted to face me. My heart started racing from his undivided attention. "I don't think I'm capable of letting you go again, Petal."

"Then don't," I said.

Hamilton was on me in an instant. His body pressed me into the couch, his soft lips crashing into mine with greedy intent. I threaded my hands in his hair and lifted my leg. I curled around him and moaned.

"Don't leave me again. No more goodbyes, Hamilton." My whispered plea between kisses stopped him in his tracks.

"Are you prepared for the level of obsession I feel for you, Petal? You're all set up at your new school, your new place to live with your professor. And I don't think I have it in me to be a part-time boyfriend. I don't think I can half-ass this with you."

Instead of commenting on his obsession, I teased him. "You're such a fucking stalker."

He smiled and pressed his nose to my collarbone. "You didn't think I let you go, did you? I might not be good enough for you, but I sure as hell was going to make sure you were alright."

I let out a huff of annoyance. "I can handle myself, you know."

"Oh, Petal," he murmured. "I learned that on the side of Highway 47."

I blushed and kissed his lips. That was one of the most empowering moments of my life. I'd never taken control like that. "Did you like that?" I asked.

"Fuck yeah, I liked that. I've never had something precious that was just my own," Hamilton said before tugging my thong down. I had to lift up off the couch to help him ease it off of my hips. "My family has always stolen the things most important to me."

Hamilton continued to sink down my body, taking my thong with him. He moved until his knees were on the floor and flimsy fabric was tossed to the side. "I'm not going anywhere, Hamilton. But you have to promise to never lie to me again. And the martyr bullshit has to stop. There is no one more perfect for me than yo—"

I couldn't finish my declaration because in a single move he had my legs pried open, one foot perched on the floor, the other stretched out on the length of the couch. His mouth found my cunt, and his tongue, oh God, his tongue lavished my wet slit until it landed on my clit.

"Fuck," I cursed.

"I missed this. Let's see how quickly I can make you come," Hamilton replied before circling my nub with his mouth. Groans. Sucking. I writhed on the leather couch as cool air danced along my skin, and his hot mouth worshiped my clit.

Hamilton's hands gripped my hips. I squirmed, my arousal so fucking intense that I could feel the anticipation of my orgasm pulse through my core. Coaxing. Tempting. "Just like that," I rasped when he started pressing harder with the tip of his tongue.

Hamilton let out a dark, needy huff. "Paint my face, Petal. I want to taste you for days."

"I think I'm in love with your mouth," I whimpered as he groaned and licked and sucked and worked me to that sweet spot of bliss.

"You think?" He stopped, teasing me. Testing me. "If you're not sure, Petal, then maybe I should stop."

I grabbed the collar of his shirt and yanked him toward me as I sat up. Planting both feet on the ground, I spread open my legs even wider and pushed him back down on my desperate cunt. Hamilton merely chuckled before finishing what he started.

My screams bounced off the walls of his new home. I tossed my head back, molten heat flooding my core as every muscle in my body tensed and then relaxed. Hamilton rode out my climax with his mouth dutifully on my clit, lapping up every drop of my decadent pleasure.

"Why the hell did I push you away when all this time we could have been fucking?" he asked as I helped him strip out of his clothes.

The rush of pleasure subsided for a moment, and I bit my lip while gathering up my courage. I must have looked nervous, because Hamilton stopped unbuttoning his shirt to look at me. "What's wrong?"

"You know I'll always believe you, right? When you say you're sorry, I know you mean it. When you say you won't do it again, I know you'd do everything in your power to avoid hurting me again."

Hamilton's shoulders slumped, and I stood up from the couch, my legs still shaking. Pressing my fingers under his chin, I lifted his head up to look at me. "I don't forgive you because I'm a forgiving person, Hamilton. I forgive you because I believe you. I believe in you."

I knew that Hamilton needed people to believe him. So many times, the people in his life turned him away when he needed them most. He just wanted to be understood. He just wanted control and acceptance.

Hamilton's eyes filled with unshed tears, and he looked up at me as if I were the most important thing in his life. I felt the sincerity in his gaze. Wrapping his arms around me, Hamilton and I stayed like that for a while. With him on his knees before me, and me standing there naked. His strong arms held me tight, and I imagined a life without his need for revenge. A life where we could just be us.

"You make me feel so worthy, Petal," he whispered before standing up.

Slowly, I helped him out of his pants, his briefs, his reservations. We walked hand in hand to his bedroom, a dark masculine space with satin sheets, dark, modern furniture, and a king sized bed.

We both eased onto the mattress and began kissing again, the taste of my pleasure heavy on his tongue. I didn't care. We found each other at the bottom of a deep kiss as our tongues clashed. Our bodies moved like crashing waves in the ocean. Closer. I just needed to be closer to this man.

We'd had sex plenty of times since we met that fateful night, but nothing ever felt this important. Nothing ever felt this meaningful and beautiful and life changing. "Protecting you. Pleasing you. It's my only purpose in life, Petal," he whispered before laying me down and settling on top of me. "I want you on top of me. Beneath me. But more importantly, I want you always next to me."

Hamilton slid inside with a single thrust. I felt completely exposed to him. My heart pounded. The friction between our skin made every nerve ending in my body light up at the feel of him. He peppered kisses along my flushed chest. Each breath felt like a harsh crescendo, leading to the pinnacle of our relationship.

My legs twitched. Swelling. Building. Hamilton looked me in the eye and made the most important declaration of our lives. "I love you, Petal."

It wasn't the first time he'd said that to me, but it was the first time I believed myself to be capable of deserving that love. "I believe you," I replied, because that was what my man craved most. He just wanted someone to hear the words spilling from his lips and accept them as true. "I love you too, Hamilton."

He caressed my body, dragging his lips along my collarbone, my neck, my jaw. I squeezed his ass, urging him to move faster. Harder.

"Deeper, Hamilton. I need you deeper. Harder. I want to feel only you." He thrust like it was all he knew. We shook the bed. We moaned and cried out. I'd never felt so alive. Pleasure burst from my sex like a loaded gun. Fast. Powerful. I gripped his back and cried out his name.

"Hamilton."

And when he came, my name was just a whisper, a reverent prayer on his soft lips. "Petal. I love you, Petal."

15

HAMILTON

 woke up to my phone vibrating on the nightstand. Vera was asleep on my chest, looking like a fucking angel with her brown hair fanned out all over my skin. I didn't even care that I was uncomfortable or that we were so wrapped up in one another that I barely got three hours of sleep. This was the fucking life. I'd wake up like this every single goddamn day if I was able to.

I wanted Vera to live with me.

The thought came out of the blue, but once my mind came up with the idea, I latched onto it. I liked having her in my space. I liked having her in my bed. I loved having Vera Garner all to myself. I was the kind of man that was all or nothing. We'd been building to this moment, and once I knew what I wanted, I went for it. Fuck anything that stood in my way—

Including myself.

Once I was done playing dress up and trying to bring down my father, I was packing her bag and forcing her to move in with me. Something told me she wouldn't mind too much.

"What are you thinking about?" she asked while tracing circles along my chest with her finger.

"The future," I replied. I wasn't going to tell her just yet.

"Does that future involve me?" she asked.

"Of fucking course it does." I stroked her hair and bit my lip, thinking about how I was going to word this.

My vibrating phone danced along my nightstand, ruining the moment. I was going to spill some sentimental words mapping out how every goddamn day of my life better have her in it. Rolling my eyes, I carefully shifted to pick it up. The moment I saw my father's name on the caller ID, I groaned.

"Mmm, who is it?" Vera asked, her sleepy voice too sexy for words.

"Jack..." I replied while staring at my phone for a lingering moment. The call went to voicemail, and I felt consumed with heavy relief.

"I didn't see him last night," Vera said. "Was he even there?"

It started ringing again before I could answer her. "He left after talking to Joseph," I explained. Vera sat up, her breasts free and marked up from my kisses last night. Little hickeys covered her soft skin. I wanted a picture of her bruised tits to frame on my wall.

"You should probably answer that," she said, her voice rough from sleep.

"He can wait. I'm doing something important with my girl." Once I answered the phone, all of the shit I was responsible for would hit me full stop. She leaned over and kissed my neck with sweet tenderness. "Petal," I whispered reverently. The idea of destruction threatened to rip me from this peaceful moment.

"I love it when you call me your girl. Almost as much as when you call me Petal," she whispered.

When Vera called me out on my bullshit that day with Saint, she told me that when you love someone, you let them bloom. And fuck, if it meant waking up to her beautiful smile, I'd water her with the blood of my enemies. I was a damn romantic now. I was whipped. Tethered. Tied up about this determined girl.

My phone rang again. "Answer the phone so we can face this together." She moved to sit beside me and rest her head on my shoulder as my phone rang a fourth—maybe fifth—time. I'd lost count. "Answer it, Hamilton."

I obeyed her and answered the call, making sure to put it on speaker phone so she could hear. There would be no more secrets between us. "Hello?"

"Hamilton!" Jack boomed. "Where were you last night? People expect to see you at these functions, and Joseph spent a lot of time with one of our distributors."

"People expect to see you at these things, too. Where have you been? You disappeared like a pussy when Joseph called you on your shit," I snapped back.

Jack sputtered. "I wasn't feeling well last night. I had to leave unexpectedly."

I resisted the urge to roll my eyes and call him

out for fucking his former daughter-in-law. I wasn't sure if Vera knew just how close they'd gotten, and I didn't want her to find out from eavesdropping on a call with Jack. I'd tell her as soon as I hung up. "Right. Well, I figured it wasn't that important to you. Something came up that I just didn't want to miss."

"Vera," Jack spat. The venom in his voice made me want to hang up the phone and forget the plan. I wanted to take Vera as far away from Jack Beauregard as possible. "I thought you wanted her away from all of this. What are you thinking, Hamilton? We were doing so good. She's nothing but a distraction—"

"Vera is none of your concern," I replied coolly.

"What about your revenge? We're so close to figuring out Joseph's plans. Once we have that, we can—"

"I'm still working on it. I'm still going to bring Joseph down. And if you're so concerned about what I'm doing, then maybe you should get out of bed and suit up yourself. What even are you doing, Jack? Are you working behind the scenes, or are you hiding?"

Jack cursed. "I'm doing everything I can on my end."

"You're getting your dick wet and letting me do the heavy lifting," I snapped back. Fuck Jack.

"Hamilton!"

"Tell me what distributor Joseph met with last night." I expertly made my voice sound bored. I pictured Jack in his bedroom, seething about the son he couldn't quite control. It felt good. Too good. For the first time in weeks, I felt like myself again. I didn't live for his praise. I lived for myself.

"Gunder Industries. They're a supplier. Theo Gunder is their CEO."

"What about Gary Herbert?"

Jack waited a beat before responding. "Gary isn't involved. Stop following that lead. I know Gary. And I've been in the business longer than you have."

"I suppose you don't need me then, Jack. Seems you've got everything figured out."

"Don't be stupid. I thought you were going to put in the work? I thought you wanted to take Joseph down?"

I let out a huff. "Tell me, Jack, what kind of man pits his sons against one another instead of handling his business on his own? One call. That's all it would take for you to shut this down. But you're a coward. You've got so many skeletons in your closet that you don't know where to begin." I'd known this whole plan was bullshit from the beginning. I entered the wolves' den but would ruin them from inside the pack.

"I don't have time to explain to you all the reasons we have to handle this quietly. I don't want to threaten you, Hamilton. But you have a very obvious weakness I'm not afraid to exploit."

My chest pounded. "I'm not afraid of you."

"You should be. If I go down, I'm taking everyone with me. Lilah. Vera. Joseph. And especially you. We're going to clean up this mess and move on. Now stop being your usual fuck up self and listen to me. Joseph was talking to Gunder Industries."

"And why is it a big ordeal that Joseph spent the evening chatting with them?" I was losing my patience but playing along.

"Because Gunder Industries is based out of San Francisco," Jack replied, his tone insistent. "There were lots of photographs of them taken together at the event. This is our lead." I looked at Vera. Her eyes were full of concern, and there was the most beautiful scowl on her pretty face. She thought Jack was as full of shit as I did. Jack continued. "Come over. We need to strategize and talk with my team."

"Yeah. I think I'm going to start working with a new team," I replied lazily before leaning over to kiss the worry right off my girl's face.

Jack raged. "What? Hamilton, you can't include other people in this. The more people that know, the more likely—"

"I don't care who knows, Jack," I replied easily. "I don't care if you threaten me. I don't care about this job or the money. My only motivation is to take Joseph down. And most importantly, I no longer care who gets caught in the crossfire, either."

"You can't do this!"

"Sucks, doesn't it?" I asked. "Trusting the wrong son." Vera smiled encouragingly at me, and it was all I needed to slam the door on Jack. She and I were in this together. Fuck anyone else. "Have a lovely day, Jack."

Hanging up the phone felt damn good. Vera cleared her throat. I pushed her down into the mattress and started kissing her like a starved man. She was so soft, so perfect, so fucking mine.

"Can we talk about what just happened?" she asked as I adored her tits.

"Sure," I replied before frantically prying her legs open and settling between them. She smelled like sex cologne. She felt warm and wet and—

"I don't want to talk about your dad while you're fucking me, Hamilton," she complained.

I nipped at her skin and teased her entrance with

the head of my cock, bumping her and sliding my hands up and down her body. "Good point," I agreed. I didn't want to think about him. "Let's talk later, then."

"You're impossible," Vera said before digging her fingers into my ass and guiding me inside of her. I threw my head back and grunted.

"You're perfect," I murmured.

I needed to clear my mind and think of only her. So I forgot about the call and spent the next hour pretending shit wasn't about to hit the fan.

In an hour, I'd meet defeat with open arms and challenge it. I'd tear apart my father's reasons for pulling me into the deep end when, for the majority of my life, he's been disappointed by me. In an hour, I'd challenge the brother who broke me, and work with the brother who terrorized my girl in the name of revenge. In an hour, I'd call my best friend and grovel—apologize for being a martyr.

But right now? I was with my girl.

Right now, I was okay.

16

HAMILTON

"So you're not really working with Jack?" Vera asked.

"I might be really stupid when it comes to being a boyfriend, but I'm not a complete idiot," I teased back. She tensed a little at the word *boyfriend*, but not in an apprehensive way. She bit her lip to force back a broad grin at my subtle declaration before continuing.

"So you're a double agent, huh?"

"Something like that. Or at least, I was. It was a very short-lived endeavor. Apparently, I'm not good at pretending to be cordial with Jack. Just like he's not good at pretending to want to take down his favorite son. I just need to figure out why he wanted me involved."

"It does feel off," she admitted.

"Jack tried appealing to my need for revenge and offered to keep you safe. I figured what better way to get information? But he's being suspiciously hands off. Saint thinks..." I let my voice trail off. It felt wrong to talk about my half brother to Vera. He stalked her. Terrified her.

"You can talk about Saint to me, Hamilton. I know he's your brother and that you're working together. I'm okay. I promise." She looked so brave right then that I wanted to carry her back to bed and reward her for it.

"The moment Jack made me that offer, I called Saint and told him what was up. He's here in DC right now ready to talk. Saint's been pulling information on one of his investors."

Vera moved to sit on my kitchen island, her bare legs folded under her and her wild hair put up in an unruly bun on top of her head.

"Invite him over. I don't like him. And I'm

probably never going to go out of my way to hang out with the guy, but he's got connections and seems like he can sniff out a story." Vera looked at me and took a deep breath. "Jess is on her way, too, by the way. I suggest you grovel." Vera stuck her hand into a cereal box before plopping some Cheerios into her mouth and nervously chewing on them. I never imagined I'd be jealous of cereal, but here we were.

"Jess is here?" I asked, suddenly fucking nervous. There was no way I'd make it out of here alive. My best friend was bound to be pissed that I ignored her for the last few weeks.

"And she spent the night with Jared. She's in a terrible mood. I currently have"—she paused to check her phone beside her—"seventy-three messages from her explicitly telling me how she's going to murder me and hide the body."

"If she's threatening bodily harm, then that means she loves you," I replied. She loved me so much that I practically had a foot in the grave. "Since when did you get so close?"

"Since Thanksgiving. I realized I needed backup bringing you in. I was done being mad at her for knowing about Saint. And I needed a friend. I still can't believe Jack and Mom are fucking. Disgusting."

The only thing worse than her being my niece

would be her being my fucking stepsister. Our family is a dumpster fire. "So you know?" I asked. "Jack claims he's keeping her around because she has information about Joseph."

Vera took another handful of Cheerios and ate them. With her mouth adorably full, she replied, "What do you think is worse, stepbrother or niece?" I looked at my girl and laughed. Even though I joked about getting off on the forbidden nature of our relationship, I didn't actually want her to have any reason to leave. The world was a fucking cruel place, and I knew a lot of people who would love to pick apart our taboo relationship. Losing Vera wasn't an option, and my only comfort was that Jack probably wouldn't marry Lilah. He was too adverse to scandal. She shook her head. "The divorce isn't even final, right? Jack is like *old* old."

"I was supposed to go to San Francisco to see what Joseph was up to, but when I got there, Joseph was waiting for me. I think your mom told him I was coming," I replied.

Vera ate more Cheerios. "That sounds about right. I wouldn't put it past her to do something like that. But why?"

"Maybe she wants Joseph back?" I offered.

"Then she's doing a shitty job of it. Fucking Jack

and helping Joseph," Vera murmured, the judgment dripping from her lips.

"What if Joseph told her to get close to Jack..." I whispered. "What if she's..."

"A double agent?" Vera supplied.

"Never thought I'd have something in common with Lilah Beauregard," I replied before letting out a low whistle. "This isn't going to end well for her." Vera winced, and I felt like shit for saying that. Regardless of everything that happened, my girl had a big, beautiful heart and was determined to keep her mother safe.

"My mom makes her own bed," Vera replied before wiping her hands off and getting off the island. I watched her go to the sink to wash off, and I went over to stand behind her.

"Hey," I began. "It's going to be okay."

She relaxed against me. "I know. You can want better for someone, but you can't force it on them."

I kissed her neck, her shoulder, I ran my palms up and down her stomach. "I'm proud of you," I whispered.

Vera turned to face me. "What for?"

I cupped her cheek and leaned in to kiss her forehead before responding. "You don't let your mother's shit dictate your life anymore."

Vera was just about to respond when the front door opened. Shit, I should have locked it. I winced. "Hamilton Beauregard, you have so much explaining to do!" Jess's voice roared.

Vera giggled. "That's my cue. Text Saint. He can come over, and we can figure this out," she replied before spinning me around and kissing me on the cheek. Devious little devil. She practically sprinted out of the room, not wanting to witness the ass kicking my best friend was about to give me.

Jess stormed toward me, wearing black sweats and an oversized shirt that said Pussy Power. She looked wired and tense. She was geared up for a massive fight. "This house is fucking ugly. You mean to tell me you've been here this entire time? And how come I throw some pussy your way and all of a sudden you're feeling more talkative, but when your best friend of two decades tries to call you over and over, I get sent to voicemail? As always, you're thinking with your dick and—"

I let out a huff and walked to Jess for a hug. I knew it would probably just piss her off even more, but I was glad she was here, and fuck it all, I didn't want to do this shit alone anymore. "I missed you," I whispered before wrapping my arms around her and patting her back. It took a moment, but she finally hugged me back while grumbling.

"You are seriously the most melodramatic asshole I've ever had the displeasure of knowing. Pushing us away for what? No cap, Hamilton. This is some bullshit."

"I love you too, Jess," I replied while continuing to hold her. The longer we hugged, the more her muscles relaxed.

"You patronizing asshole. You selfish bastard."

"You're such a good friend," I replied. She sniffled. Tears were never good.

"You could have told me." Jess pulled back and wiped at her tears. The thick eyeliner around her eyes was smeared, and she looked tired. Her shirt was wrinkled. "And where is Vera? While she was getting dicked, I had to spend the night with Jared. That dude is hilarious but should probably be on some predator watch list or some shit. I woke up to him jacking off in the bed beside mine."

I scowled. I wasn't just possessive with the girl that had my heart. Fuck Jared for getting a sleepover with my bestie, too. "I'm still not clear on why Jared was involved at all."

Jess rolled her eyes. "We wouldn't have had to chat with him if you would have answered, like, any of my calls." Jess's voice was rough and deep from lack of sleep. "He got Vera tickets to the auction. Did he kiss her? That was part of the deal. I really hope he tongued her hard. Fucking bullshit."

Rage that had been simmering under the surface roared to life. Oh, yeah. I was still massively pissed about that. "I saw the kiss," I growled.

"Serves you right," Jess replied triumphantly. "So we're done with the bullshit now? When are you coming home?"

"We can't leave just yet," I admitted while guiding my best friend over to the living room to sit down—after kicking Vera's panties under the couch.

"I'm figuring out what Jack and Joseph are up to."

"What the fuck else is new. Once again, Hamilton is running around trying to destroy his family instead of just living his life. Typical," Jess replied before kicking off her boots and putting her feet up on the coffee table. It felt good having my best friend in my space. It made everything feel more like mine. "You're working with Jack now? How the hell did that even happen?"

"Some mild threats and an opportunity to take down my brother."

"How disgustingly predictable," Jess replied. "I'm assuming you didn't take the bait, though." Jess shook her head in frustration. "So this is just another revenge thing?" Her voice sounded bitter.

"Not exactly. I mean yeah, it is. But it's also—"

"Also what? I just want to hear you say it out loud."

I heard the bathroom door open and close. "It's not just revenge."

"Then what the fuck else is it? Cause where I'm standing, it looks like you put your girlfriend and best friend through hell just so you could go rogue Batman all up on Jack and Joseph," Jess countered. It was like cornering a motherfucking tiger.

"I can't be everything I need to be for Vera until this is done. If you can't respect or understand that, then fine."

Vera emerged from the hallway, her brown hair wet and a pair of my sweats rolled up at her waist and ankles. My shirt swallowed her curves, but my dick was already twitching at the sight of my girl in my clothes. So what if I'm a fucking caveman?

"Jared is a fucking sleep talker, Vera," Jess growled. "And he choked the rooster in the middle of the night. With me in the damn room."

"Sorry I didn't come home last night. Hamilton and I needed to talk and—"

"Talk? You look like you got slapped upside the

head with dick, Vera. We are going to have to discuss this later, though, because I'm still bitch slapping Hamilton. Back to the previous conversation. So, you don't think you can be fully present in your relationship until you get revenge on your brother and Jack?"

Vera's carefree face fell. Fuck, Jess. Way to not hold back.

I swallowed. "You don't get it."

"I get it. I just want to make sure you're being honest with yourself, Hamilton. Don't tell me this is for Vera when it's not. You want revenge. Plain and simple."

"And what's wrong with that?!" I roared. Jess didn't even flinch. Vera looked like she wanted to cry. "You know what they did to me. You know what they're capable of."

"I'm just saying, if you're fine with putting your best friend and your girl in the crossfire of your vendetta, then whatever. I just want to make it very, very clear what you're doing and what you've risked."

I inhaled and exhaled, my emotions all over the place. Maybe Jess was right. Maybe I shouldn't be going after Jack and Joseph. I could walk away.

"Enough," Vera said while looking at Jess with

fierce, protective eyes. "I love you, Jess. Feel your feels, but I won't sit here and let you talk to him this way. If Hamilton wants to burn the Beauregard empire down to the ground, I'm with him. If he wants to walk away, I'm with him. If he has moments of weakness, I'm with him. If he wants to be with me, I'm with him. If he doesn't want to be with me, I'll track his ass down, blow him on the side of a public highway and remind him that I'm just as stubborn as he is. Don't sit here and ask Hamilton what he's willing to lose for revenge. Tell him you'll stay regardless of what he chooses."

My dick stood at attention, proud as fuck of my girl. "Shit. I want to fuck you so bad right now," I murmured. Jess rolled her eyes, but otherwise seemed speechless from Vera's little declaration.

"Looks like I walked into a party," Saint said. I turned my head to stare at him. "Hope you don't mind, the door was unlocked."

Saint wore a pastel bow tie, suspenders, and bright green pants. His hair was slicked back, and he had a laptop under his arm. I stood up and walked over to Vera, who looked like she needed some support. Her eyes were wide as she took in my brother, all the false bravado from her earlier speech gone. I patted her lower back affectionately.

"Good to see you again, Vera," Saint said, his tone cautious. Saint liked to act like a cocky bastard, but he wasn't a total dick. More importantly, he was perceptive. Saint knew that if he wanted to be in my life, he'd have to fix shit with my girl.

"You here to help?" Vera asked.

Jess fumed on the couch. Saint smirked and walked over to us. My worlds were all colliding.

"I'm here to bring them down." He held out his hand for Vera to shake, and she looked at it with a beat of trepidation before finally shaking it. We were mad. Hurting. Healing.

But we were together.

Family was the motherfuckers you chose, after all.

17

My mother looked good. Surprisingly good. Rosy cheeks, a grin despite sitting across from her estranged daughter. Her designer outfit was tight on her skinny body, but from what I could see, she wasn't sickly looking anymore. At least she'd ordered a cobb salad, so I knew she was eating again.

"You look great, Mom," I said before lifting the glass of sparkling water to my lips and taking a sip. It felt weird sitting casually across from her at a nice café back in Connecticut. I forced myself not to look over her shoulder at Saint, who was in disguise and sitting at a booth beside us. Hamilton insisted on coming to this meeting should anything happen, but Mom would have recognized him immediately and fled. We all decided it was best he stay in DC to follow Joseph around.

Saint offered to step in, seeing as he was a little too good at blending in when he wanted to. The fact that I trusted him to protect me said a lot about how much had changed in the last couple of days. The crazy journalist was sitting in a booth, sipping on coffee and wearing a beanie. His grunge look was completely different than his usual hipster-preppy style. He blended effortlessly. It made me wonder how many times he managed to follow me without me realizing it.

"I feel great," she replied. "Or at least I did. Until you called and practically blackmailed me into this meeting. Before that, it had been nice to focus on myself and not worry about anyone else." The dig wasn't subtle or productive, but I let her have this win. The space from her was good for me too, if I were being honest. Now that I wasn't focused on my mother's happiness, I could focus on my own.

"I know the feeling," I replied with a smile before grabbing a dinner roll and taking a bite out of it. "And I didn't blackmail you. Don't be dramatic. I just asked how your relationship scheme with Jack was going and invited you to lunch."

Instead of commenting on the opaque blackmail I'd tossed her way, she commented on my eating habits. Typical. "Slow down on the carbs. You won't keep Hamilton's attention if you keep stuffing your face."

I nearly choked on my food. Of course she knew about Hamilton and me. Jack probably told her when Hamilton cut him off a couple of days ago. I just wasn't expecting her to be so open about it. Was she mad? Was she going to tell me to break up with him? I scowled at myself for ever giving a fuck. "Hamilton likes the way I stuff my face," I replied with a wink. God, it felt good not to care anymore.

"Don't be so crass," Mom snapped. She looked me up and down once more. "I hate this."

"Hate what?" I asked.

"We're so estranged. It's weird. Where did we go wrong, Vera?"

I wondered where she was going with this conversation. Was she trying to reconcile with me? Was it wrong to hope? "I think pinpointing where we went wrong would require a level of self-awareness you don't possess, Mom."

"Again with the snappy remarks. The daughter I raised would never talk back to me."

"The daughter you raised was miserable," I replied with a frown.

She shook her head. "This is ridiculous. But I came here for a reason, Vera. I want to talk to you about this relationship with Hamilton. Though I'm not sure you'll listen. Jack seems to think I can talk some sense into you."

"How is Jack, by the way?" I asked, brow arched challengingly as I fought the urge to squirm in my seat. "You're still staying at his house, aren't you?"

Mom picked up her glass and took a long gulp. I kept my eyes locked on her. "Yes," she replied before smoothing her soft, silk, button up shirt. "I'm still staying there. Not that you care, because the suffering of your mother means nothing to you. But, thanks to the divorce and everything leading up to it, I'm not sure I'll be getting anything. It's taking me a while to get on my feet."

The words poured out of me without warning. "It's hard to get back on your feet if you stay on your back, Mom," I replied.

She grabbed the cloth napkin in her lap and

tossed it on the table. "I don't have to sit here and listen to this," she hissed. "I came here to help you—to warn you. And this is the thanks I get? I don't even know you anymore."

She came here to help me? What did that even mean? "That's because the Vera you know let you walk all over her." Mom fumbled for her Louis Vuitton purse, and I let out a sigh. I wasn't going to get the information I needed by insulting her. "Mom. Please sit. I'm sorry." She swept her eyes up and down my body.

She looked around the restaurant for a moment before reluctantly sitting down. "What do you want, Vera?" she replied with a huff.

I wasn't sure what I wanted from my mother. We would never get back to how we were, and more importantly, I didn't want to go back to how we were. Looking back, I'd always taken a back seat to my mother's life and whims. Yes, she worked hard to give me a roof over my head and pushed me to do well in school, but we were still toxic. Mom was just a child raising a child. But we were grown now, and I had a say in what I wanted to do with my life.

I didn't tell her this, though.

"I want us to be better," I replied. It was the truth. "I want a relationship with you, Mom. Things have changed between us, yes, but that doesn't mean we can't still talk and try to be cordial."

Mom picked up her fork and squeezed the handle tightly. "It does feel weird to not talk to you. We've always been so close," she replied before blinking away tears and looking away. "I understand that you're determined to do things your own way. I'm disappointed that we're at this point, but I understand. Sometimes mothers don't always get it right."

"Daughters don't always get it right either," I relented. We all had our parts in this.

"You know, the day I left my mother's trailer, she threw hot coffee at me," Mom whispered in a faraway voice. She never really talked about her childhood, her mother, or her mother's boyfriend. I was so young when we got out of that situation that I never experienced the abuse firsthand. It was one of the reasons I was thankful for Mom. She was brave enough to leave, and that completely changed the trajectory of my life.

Mom continued. "She was furious. Blamed me for her failing relationship. She claimed that I asked for his attention." I watched as my mother broke a little bit more. Her hands trembled. Her shoulders slumped. "I've had a lot of time to think these last few weeks, and I realized that I was doing the exact same thing to you, blaming you for my failed relationship when you weren't to blame. I'm sorry for that, Vera."

To say that I was shocked that she admitted that would be an understatement. I reached across the table and grabbed Mom's hand. "It's okay. I forgive you."

Mom cleared her throat. "It's a nasty cycle, isn't it?"

"What is?"

"We all become our parents in the end."

I shook my head. "No. That's not true. I'm my own person. You're your own person. Hamilton is nothing like Jack, either—"

"You need to stay away from Hamilton, Vera," Mom whispered.

"This again?" How could we go from having such a good conversation to this again? I thought that since she'd left Joseph, she'd be done with this. "Is this because you're with Jack?"

Mom shook her head. "No. No. Jack isn't going to marry me. I'm just staying because...never mind. I just think you need to stay away from Hamilton and stay out of this business with Joseph, too."

I narrowed my eyes at her. "What do you know about Hamilton and Joseph, Mom?"

I watched as she started looking around the restaurant. Slowly, I watched my mother transform into the woman she was when she was married to Joseph. Terrified. Timid. What was happening? "I know that you are in way over your head. You have no idea what Jack's planning."

"What does that even mean?" I asked.

Mom bit her lip nervously. "I've already said too much." I watched as she leaned back in her chair and crossed her arms over her chest.

"Tell me what you know, Mom."

She bit her nail. "I know that you shouldn't associate with Hamilton right now."

"Why?"

"Because I don't want you sucked into this mess."

"Why?" I pressed on. Mom squirmed. Had she always looked so helpless? "Mom. Break the cycle. Tell me what's going on. You love me, Mom. You care about me. You want me to be safe. Just tell me."

She shook her head and started breathing heavily. "If I tell you, you have to promise not to tell anyone," she whispered. "I'm serious, Vera."

I lied easily. "I won't say a word. Now tell me why I need to stay away from Hamilton."

"Jack is trying to get rid of Hamilton," she whispered before leaning closer. "When Hamilton went to San Francisco, there was supposed to be some sort of hit man waiting for him."

My eyes widened. I clutched my chest and felt the rapid way my breathing turned erratic. "What? Why? How?" I stuttered.

"Do you know how the Beauregards got so rich?" she asked. "It's funny, really. Ironic."

"How?" I asked.

"Unless some cheap woman lies about a pregnancy, they marry into money. Jack was close to losing everything before he proposed to Nikki. His family had businesses failing left and right."

"Nikki," I whispered.

"She had sole control over seventy percent of the Beauregard fortune. Lucky bitch. She was an heiress, you know. Only child. And she inherited a fuck ton of money when her parents died. Last year, a new will showed up anonymously on Jack's doorstep. Can you believe it? The woman has been dead for years and suddenly someone is blackmailing Jack with it. Guess who Nikki wanted to give it all to. Not her son. Not her husband. A bastard."

I sat back in my seat while trying to piece it together. "What about Joseph?" I asked.

"Joseph is playing a game of his own," Mom whispered. "I got scared, and I told Joseph what Jack was planning. I guess Joseph intervened somehow, saving Hamilton's life."

"So Jack wants to have Hamilton killed, and Joseph knows that Nikki's entire fortune is being left to someone else?"

"I don't know all the details. I just know that Hamilton was supposed to be killed the moment he got off that plane." A waiter walked by carrying a tray, putting a brief pause to our conversation.

"You don't know why Jack wanted Hamilton to work for the company and find a laundering scheme?" I pressed. "If Jack wanted his son killed, he could have easily done it. Why go through all these hoops?"

Mom nervously trembled. "I'm not sure. I already know too much, Vera. I should have never stayed with Jack. I'm trapped. I'm scared to leave, scared to stay."

I sat there, absorbing the words pouring from my mother's mouth in shock. Holy shit. I needed to warn Hamilton. "Mom, you have to get out of Jack's house," I whispered.

"I can't. Jack is willing to kill his own son. What

do you think he would do to me for knowing this? For warning you?"

"Come with me. I can get you somewhere safe. Okay? You don't have to do this—"

Mom straightened her spine. "I'm fine. I'm a survivor, baby. I just don't want you wrapped up in this. Promise me you'll stop seeing Hamilton."

I stood up and looked down at my mother. "Thank you for letting me know," I whispered. I didn't have time to argue with her.

"What are you going to do?" Mom asked.

Once again, I lied easily. "Nothing. I'm going to stay away from Hamilton."

She sighed in relief. "I'll call you once I'm out, okay? Jack won't hurt me. He doesn't know that I know anything."

I politely nodded. There was no way in fucking hell that Mom would stay another night with Jack Beauregard. The moment I left this café, I'd go to the police.

Saint had already paid his bill and was waiting outside on the sidewalk or me. I struggled to breathe, to think. "I'll call you, okay?" I promised Mom.

"Be safe," she replied. This felt like a turning

point. The bar was practically on the floor, but at least my mother didn't want me dead.

I patted the recording device strapped to my chest and sighed. "Sorry, Mom," I whispered before walking outside.

18

HAMILTON

I marched into Joseph's office without a single fuck. I didn't even take the time to come to terms with the fact that my actual father wanted to fucking kill me. I was a man on a mission. Joseph was sitting at his desk and playing on his phone. The large windows in his office had a picturesque view of DC. His ornate antique desk was oversized—like his ego.

I was reeling. I knew Jack was up to something,

but I never imagined it was this. Killing me? Was he honestly capable of that? When Vera called me sobbing, it took me a while to make out what she was saying. Saint had to take the phone from her trembling hands and give me a summary of what Lilah had said. Vera coordinated the meeting with her mother, hoping to get some information we could use.

But what she came back with was so much worse.

"Can I help you?" Joseph asked before looking up at me for a brief moment. "You look like shit. What are you, a lumberjack? Flannel doesn't look good on you."

I ignored his comment. Of course I looked like shit. I'd had a shitty couple of days. "Why'd you do it?" I came here for one reason and one reason only: to figure out why my abusive brother would bother to save my life.

"You'll have to be more specific," he replied in a bored tone before setting down his phone and adjusting his cufflinks.

"Did you save my life in San Francisco?"

Joseph grinned. "Ah, so you found out dear old dad wants to kill you, huh?" He sat up. "I mean, that's pretty intense, right? When Lilah called, I almost didn't believe it." I paced the floors, my boots dragging across his expensive rug as my brother looked on with glee. "I suppose yours is the worse fate. Dad just wanted to send me to prison for my little extracurriculars. He wants you six feet under."

"What are you talking about?" I gritted before sitting in the leather chair opposite his desk.

"It's obvious." He pulled out one of his desk drawers and produced a bottle of whiskey and two crystal glasses. "Want a drink, brother?"

I sure as fuck needed a drink, but this wasn't some bullshit brotherly bonding moment. "No. Just tell me what's going on."

"I've been working with a business partner. He uses Beauregard Industries to funnel some money, and I get a cut. But you already know this, don't you?"

Hearing my brother speak so plainly about his illegal activities felt...wrong and anticlimactic. It sent a ripple of disappointment through me. "Yeah. I do." There was no point in lying now.

"Jack found out a few months ago and got jealous. He wanted a piece of the pie. But you know what, Hamilton? I've been sharing my entire goddamn life. What's a couple million for myself?"

Joseph poured himself a drink and took a sip. My

veins thudded with adrenaline and fury. "So, what, Jack got jealous?" I asked.

"He got vengeful. He claimed I was risking his job. But really, I think he was just pissed that I had the balls to think outside the box." Joseph tapped his temple, shaking loose his styled blond hair. "You'd love my business associate. He's in the business of selling women to men with particular kinks."

I frowned. "Disgusting, but keep talking."

"Think about it. You're on my trail and suddenly get murdered? Jack was going to pin it on me. He had all the evidence he needed. You had all the reason in the world to chase me down. I had the motive to end your life. All the ducks were in a row." He punctuated his words by clapping his hands together. "But he wasn't planning on Lilah." Joseph grinned to himself. "That bitch finally came in handy."

"Jack wouldn't risk the scandal," I replied.

"Wouldn't he, though?" Joseph asked. "Billions of dollars, a cushy retirement. And last I heard, he really enjoyed getting his dick sucked by my ex-wife. With me out of the way, he could probably breeze right over the humiliation of marrying her. Would probably spin it in the press that they fell in love while he mourned. A fucking fairy tale. Too bad his new girlfriend loves me more."

Joseph set down his glass of whiskey, and I reached across the desk to grab it. Fuck it. I needed a drink. The burning liquid went down my throat, and I hissed in appreciation. Naturally, the shit was smooth and expensive as fuck. "He was going to kill me."

"And you just walked right into that trap. It's embarrassing. Honestly, Hamilton. Do you have any sense of self-preservation? Spending an entire evening with you at the nightclub was brutal, but I suppose it was worth it to not be framed for murder. I was smart, too. Made sure the tabloids got photographs of us with those models."

"Why didn't you tell me?" I asked.

"Would you have listened to me? We don't work together. I didn't save your ass, I saved myself." I took another gulp, and Joseph checked his phone. "You're brave to come here, you know," he murmured absentmindedly. "I have just as much of a reason to want you dead as Jack."

I rolled my eyes. "If this is about the will, you can have it. I'm not interested in claiming Mom's money." And it was the honest truth. It felt like blood money.

Jack was willing to murder me for it. I couldn't imagine any amount of money being worth that.

"You say that, but I'm not inclined to believe you. I see how much you thrived in the last few weeks. If I didn't know any better, I'd say you actually enjoyed wearing Versace suits and spending Beauregard money."

"Mom's money," I whispered.

"The weak woman who ended her life was nothing more than a ghost that lived in our home and took my pills."

It took every ounce of energy in my body to not lunge across this desk and beat the shit out of him. "Shut your goddamn mouth," I roared.

"Or what?" Joseph snapped. "I never understood your relationship. You were living, breathing evidence of Dad's infidelity." He stood up and walked over to the window, showing me his back. "I never understood it. She acted like you were the best thing to ever happen to her. When I went to the press about your birth mother, I was doing our family a favor."

As I stared at Joseph, it suddenly occurred to me that my brother was nothing more than a lonely child throwing a temper tantrum. He wanted to be the center of attention. The man that made my life a living hell suddenly seemed very, very small.

"So what's next, brother?"

I let out an exhale as he turned around to face me. I took a moment to look at Joseph, enjoying the realization that he was weak and expendable. I'd finally gotten out from under his thumb. "I suppose I owe you one," I said.

"Oh?"

"I have a flight to Connecticut in two hours. Vera and I are getting Lilah out of that house, and we're going to the police with everything, including your involvement. I don't owe you a head start, but I'm giving you one. We have the evidence we need, and if anything happens to me, Saint won't hesitate to ruin you."

"A head start?" he asked, brows raised. "I tortured you. I beat you up. I beat the shit out of you. You're seriously going to come here and warn me?" Joseph started laughing manically, his head tipped back. I watched, my face stoic. In this moment, hate felt like nothing but a shortcut. An easy way out of an impossible situation. Joseph Beauregard didn't deserve my grace. "You're weak. An embarrassment. Don't think for one second I wouldn't sit here and ruin you without a second thought. What happened to revenge? I thought that was all that motivated you these days." His angry words were accompanied by spit flying from his chapped lips.

My phone vibrated in my pocket, and I knew it was Vera texting to make sure I was okay. The quiet reminder of what was waiting for me emboldened my words and actions.

"You'll still get caught," I replied with a shrug. "You'll lose your job. Your money. Your life. You have no one. At best, you'll have nothing. At worst, you'll get caught and spend your life in prison."

Joseph's nostrils flared in anger as he checked the Rolex strapped to his wrist. "Are you done?"

I circled his desk and approached my brother, feeling stronger and lighter than I'd felt in years. "You always made it sound like being a Beauregard was the best thing a person could be," I whispered. "I always wanted to fit in. I wanted to feel a part of something. I wanted to be accepted." Joseph tipped his chin up. Beads of sweat trailed down his face. "But I've never been prouder to be nothing like you than I am in this moment."

Joseph curled his lip. "Get the fuck out of my office," he growled.

Smiling, I took a step back and made my way toward the door. "Goodbye, Joseph."

When I walked out of his office and down the hall to the elevator, I realized, for the first time in my life, that I no longer feared Joseph Beauregard. He was nothing. No one.

I pitied him.

Pulling out my phone, I quickly typed a text to Vera.

Hamilton: I'm coming home, Petal. Let's end this.

I bit my lip and paced the floors, waiting for Hamilton to show up. It had been a long day, and all I wanted was to see him, feel him. I needed reassurance that he was okay.

"You're making Little Mama nervous," Jess said from her spot on the pull-out couch. Saint was standing by the front window, peering out the wooden blinds at the hotel parking lot.

The small room we were in smelled like bleach

and cigarette smoke. I listened to the hum of the heater and the muffled sounds of a couple talking as they passed our door. I didn't want to be in this crowded double hotel room waiting for Hamilton to arrive. Every gurgling of the pipes and slamming door had me flinching with fear.

"We should be safe here. I booked the room under a fake name. Jack doesn't know Hamilton is coming back to Connecticut." He ran a hand over his gun and poked at the blinds once more. In the short time I'd gotten to know Saint, I'd come to learn that he was an observer. He was good at his job because he saw the little details that no one else did.

For example, he brought it to my attention that Mom was wearing a forty-five-thousand-dollar necklace when she met me at the café. He said it looked like something Jack had once given his mother.

I stopped my pacing to crouch low and pet Little Mama, who was obviously wondering where her human was. Jess and I drove her back here after the charity event in DC, and I'd been watching her at Anika's house. My professor loved the dog and had already bought her enough toys to last a lifetime.

Now, we were waiting at a hotel outside of town. We had a lot of shit to figure out, but more importantly, we needed to make sure Hamilton was safe from Jack. I didn't want to be sitting ducks at his townhouse. I didn't know how far Jack was willing to go. Now that Hamilton wasn't cooperating, would he just hire some fucking hit man to do the job? I knew that Jack had the kind of money to make something like that happen.

"Maybe we should just go to the police. When Hamilton gets here, we could just—"

Saint stopped staring outside to turn around and face me. "I know that what I'm about to say might come across as a bit ironic, considering my history of not giving a shit about your mother, but I don't think it's safe for Lilah if we go to the police right away."

I swallowed as Saint adjusted his tie. "Why not?"

"Jack is the governor. He has people in his pocket at every level of government. If we go to the cops before making sure your mother is away from him, there is no telling what he might do to her. Her confession is literally the only evidence that we have right now, and if I'm being honest, I'm not sure that it's enough. Hamilton wasn't wearing a wire when he went to speak with Joseph."

"Dumbass," Jess interjected while shaking her head and taking a sip of her tea.

"What do you mean it's not enough?" I asked.

"I think we need more. I just know firsthand what can happen to people that try to bring Jack down. They end up ruined."

I stopped petting Little Mama and walked over to Saint, feeling nervous about approaching the questions in my mind. "Are you referring to your mother?" I asked. "Jack told me his version of events, but I'm curious what actually happened."

"She didn't want to give up Hamilton. But she had no choice," Saint replied, his voice calm. His usually expressive face was blank, as if he'd disassociated from the memory.

"Why not?"

"Jack threatened her every way he could. He said he'd leak their relationship and ruin any job she'd ever have. He threatened to buy out my grandparents' company and run it into the ground. He told her he'd have her removed from her graduate program. Her house foreclosed on. Her entire life down the drain. He knew the only way he'd keep Nikki—and her money—was if he got my mother out of the picture."

Jack was such a puppeteer, constantly pulling the strings and controlling people to his benefit.

"That is so fucked up."

"She got married. Had me. But she always

thought about Hamilton. And when she got brave enough to come forward, Jack came through on his promise to ruin her life. Dad left her. Her boss fired her. All she's ever wanted was a relationship with Hamilton. I'm hoping that at the end of this all, he'll finally agree to meet her."

"I wouldn't hold your breath," Jess replied before leaning back on the couch and pulling a plastic baggie with a brownie out of her purse. "Anyone want an edible?"

"Fuck yes," Saint replied before leaving me at the window and taking a piece.

"No, thank you," I replied. I wanted to be completely stone cold sober when I saw Hamilton.

"Hamilton has this twisted sense of loyalty to Nikki," Jess replied. "I hope when all of this bullshit is done that he'll let go of that."

"It's not bullshit, Jess," I snapped back. I was tired of her bitching at Hamilton. Forgiveness was a gift Jess didn't possess. She was loyal to Hamilton, but still pissed at him, too.

"Yeah, yeah. I'm working on forgiving the asshole. I know it's not productive to be pissed for all eternity. I'm just scared, you know? Jack really could have killed him," Her voice hit a full stop, and a sob rattled her vocal cords. "He could have died, and he wasn't talking to me."

I stopped staring out the window and walked back over to Jess. Leaning over the back of the couch, I wrapped my arms around her and kissed her cheek affectionately. I understood it. I'd been a nervous wreck since hearing Jack's plans. "He's going to be okay. We're going to fix this."

Saint checked his phone. "I'm going to go home. A friend of mine is a hacker and has been looking into some of Jack's emails. Hopefully, we will have more evidence tomorrow. I think the best course of action is to pull as much evidence as we can together, get your mother out of there, then go to the police. Until then, Hamilton should go nowhere alone. And if he has to leave this hotel, he needs to stick to public places. He's got a target on his back, and you probably do too. This is so much bigger than a story. This is life or death. Be diligent," he instructed before nodding at me, grabbing his keys and leaving. I followed him to the door and locked it behind him.

"Well, that was ominous," Jess said before tossing her pot brownie back in the plastic baggie and cradling her head in her hands. "Fuck. Infinity keeps calling. She wants me to come home, but I don't even know what I'm going to tell her."

"The less she knows right now, the better," I replied.

Jess nodded in agreement before standing. "You'll be okay, yeah?" It wasn't like I had much of a choice. Certainly, Jack wasn't going to show up at the hotel with a gun?

"I'll be fine. Little Mama will scare off anyone who bothers me. Go see Infinity. We have a lot of work ahead of us."

Jess pulled her lips into a tight smile and patted Little Mama on the head. "See you tomorrow."

I spent the next hour waiting for Hamilton to show up at the hotel we'd gotten on the outskirts of town under Saint's fake name. We couldn't be too careful, not now that we knew there was a target on our backs.

So much had happened. It was a lot to unpack, and I wasn't even sure where to start. Mom finally came through for me. Even though I had to lie to her, I couldn't help but feel thankful that she finally cared enough about my safety to be honest. She'd been chasing money and men for a while now, but I had hope for a future where she worried about herself.

I was also obsessed with her comments about the nasty cycle we were all stuck in. The truth was, maybe it was our first instinct to follow the path we knew and become what others expected of us. But I was separating myself from the narrative. I was my own woman; I was loving my own man. I was stepping away from the toxic wasteland of this never-ending karma.

A slight knock on the hotel door made Little Mama whine, and I got up to see who it was. The moment my eyes landed on Hamilton, I let out a sigh of relief and opened the door.

He looked handsome, despite the difficult day and traveling. I reached out to grab him by his gray Henley and yanked him into the hotel room before wrapping my arms around him. "I'm so glad you're here." He rubbed my back as he squeezed me against his rock-hard body. It felt like finally inhaling again after holding my breath.

"Shit day, yeah?" he asked.

"How are you holding up?" I replied. I'd grown to understand Hamilton in the last few months, and I knew his unique coping mechanisms would need kindling after such a traumatic day.

"You know how I'm a fucking mess when shit goes down, Petal?"

I pulled away and stroked his cheek. "You're not a mess, Hamilton."

He leaned into my palm, turning his head so that my thumb brushed against his lip. "I just need you right now." His whispered words sent a tremor through me. "I don't want to think about anything but how good you squeeze my cock when you come." He ran his hand down my shoulder and arm before grabbing my waist. "I don't want to feel anything but your lips on my skin." He pulled me closer, pressing his hard cock against my core. "I don't want to talk about anything but how fucking perfect you are. I want to say dirty little nothings in your ear until sunrise, until my voice is hoarse from moaning your name."

Hamilton grabbed my ass, then lifted me up. I wrapped my legs around him as he walked me over to the hotel bed and laid me down. "And then tomorrow, I want to protect you, Petal. I want to end this so that I can spend the rest of my life worshiping your pussy, your mind, your precious soul, and your heart."

He tugged at the waistband of my leggings and with considerable effort, managed to get the tight spandex off my trembling body. I shivered from the sweet contradiction of his heated kisses and the slight chill in the air.

Hamilton reached one hand behind his back and took off his shirt with ease. I'd never get enough of his body, of his sculpted abs, is soft skin and rough touch. I lifted up slightly and unbuttoned his pants before easing them over his hips and muscular thighs.

My muscles tensed in excitement the moment I saw the outline of his hard cock through the thin material of his briefs. "I can't control myself when I'm with you. It's the most freeing feeling in the world, Petal," he whispered before rubbing his palm over his shaft.

I breathed in and out before removing my soft shirt. His eyes locked on my breasts, my nipples cutting through my sports bra in sharp little points.

"Tell me, Petal. Do you like hate fucks?"

I swallowed. The idea of Hamilton fucking me like he hated me sounded appealing. One of our hottest times together was the night he tried telling me goodbye. "Why? You want to hate me, Hamilton?" I asked slowly, my voice taunting and sensual.

"No," he whispered. "I just want to fuck all my rage into your delicate body." He leaned over and bit the inside of my thigh. "I want to break the skin. Lick up your pain. I want to work you hard, Petal."

His words shouldn't have turned me on as much as they did, but fuck, I was slick with need. Turned on so much I couldn't even function. He sucked on my skin. "I can handle it," I whispered. I wanted it all. I wanted to be the person who healed Hamilton Beauregard. I wanted to be the escape he craved.

"Good. Tell me if it becomes too much, Petal."

This sounded like I needed a fucking safe word. Hamilton grinned before licking a long line up my pussy. Slowly. Dangerously. He was like a predator prepared to pounce.

Then, Hamilton grabbed my hips and dug his fingers into my flesh. He flipped me over and then pressed me into the mattress, placing his palm in the middle of my back and holding me down.

Smack! His hand slapped across my ass. "That sound? I want to hear it over and over again," he groaned before slapping it again. I could feel my body jiggling from the harsh hit. Pain flared where his hand made contact, but it wasn't too bad.

Then, I felt his hot breath feather over me. Sharp teeth sunk into my flesh, and he sucked on my ass cheek with painful fervor. I squirmed, he held me down with his palm. I cried out, and he spread my legs before pressing his thumb at my asshole. Yeah, my asshole. I couldn't even romanticize the intimate invasion because my entire body tensed up.

"What are you doing?" I asked.

"I want to be inside every part of you."

"Don't we need to work up to that?" I asked, my voice shrill.

Hamilton pressed his thumb inside of me slightly. The stretching sensation burned, and I let out a moan. "Oh, Petal. I'll put in the work. Not tonight, but one day this pretty virgin hole will be mine."

He spit on my crack, and I felt the hot moisture mix with my slick need. His hand ran up and down my slit, pressing against my pulsing clit. "Hamilton..." I begged. Instead of giving me what I wanted, he used his free hand to tug my long hair, forcing my back to arch.

My scalp turned tender, and he dragged his teeth along my neck. I felt the head of his cock pressing against me. "You never did finish what you started. How about you be a good girl and choke on my cock, Petal?"

My heaving chest struggled to settle. He let go of my hair and laid down on his back beside me before grabbing me and forcing me on top of him, with my pussy at his lips and the head of his cock perfectly aligned with my own mouth. He moved me so effortlessly. Hamilton had all the strength, all the control.

"I want to hear you gag, Petal," he whispered before wrapping his hands around my thighs and furiously licking my clit. I moaned and trembled for a brief moment, temporarily stunned by his abrupt mouth.

Then, I sunk lower onto his cock and started pumping him in and out. He tasted salty, and his smooth skin felt good on my tongue. Obeying his wishes, I took him all the way back, deep in my throat. I gagged and choked until my eyes watered and his erection was slick with my spit and tears.

He worked me with his skilled tongue, circling my clit. It was exhausting pleasure. I felt drained and tense. I came hard and long, but Hamilton didn't stop.

I stopped sucking him to cry out. I was too sensitive. "I can't—" I choked out as he licked and licked and licked and motherfucking licked. The force of his talented tongue on my clit sent me rocking against his face.

He paused for just a moment to speak. "I'll stop

licking your pussy when you're swallowing my cum, Petal."

I gasped when he sucked on my sensitive nub, another orgasm rolling through me almost instantly. I screamed and twitched, but Hamilton didn't stop. Quickly, I started moaning and sucking his dick once more, this time, more desperate to find relief. It was all too much. My entire body was shaking from his persistent mouth.

Up and down, I moved. Moaning, sobbing, breaking from the pressure. Another orgasm. I was spent. Too much, it was too fucking much.

Finally, Hamilton let out a moan and started jerking his hips. I knew I only had a few moments before he was coming in my mouth, and I welcomed it.

Ropes of salty cum shot out against my tongue, and I swallowed it whole. Moaning in pleasure as he finally released my clit from his lips and let me bask in the multiple orgasms I'd just earned.

I toppled over and fell on my back, my head level with his thighs, my legs shaking uncontrollably. Our combined breathing was the only sound in the motel room.

"Petal, your mouth is perfect."

"Your mouth is demanding," I whispered back.

"Oh, I'm just getting started. Give me a minute and I'll be ready again."

I blinked twice and sat up on the mattress. "You're kidding."

He looked down at his cock and smirked at me. "Does it look like I'm kidding?" Hamilton sat up and shoved me onto the mattress. He pried my legs apart with his strong hands and pressed at my entrance once more. I jumped at the feel of him.

"I'm too sensitive."

"Good," he replied before kissing my neck. "That means you feel how hard you make me even more."

Hamilton spent the next ten minutes sucking on my neck, my collarbone, my breasts, my stomach, my thigh. Every chance he got, he pressed against my clit with his finger or his dick, reminding me that it was him winding me up so much. It was a painful pleasure unlike anything I'd ever experienced before. He was literally going to make me come until I physically couldn't anymore.

"Ready for me to fill you up, Petal?" he asked.

I wasn't sure how much more I could take. "Yes," I whispered.

One single thrust. Hamilton impaled me with his cock and started pumping hard, harder, harder. In and out, he rocked the bed nearly off its frame. I screamed his name, not caring who could hear us next door. Hamilton pressed his palm over my chest, holding me down as he showed me the power behind each move.

It seemed to go on for hours. He manipulated my body into various positions. Each time, he held me down, moved me whatever way he wanted and worked my body like he owned me. I felt like a precious little fuck doll. The agony of coming over and over and over again was pure bliss. I'd never been so sensitive. It was the rawest form of pleasure I'd ever experienced.

"I love you, Petal," he said like the devotion was a curse. "I love you. Only you. I fucking love you, fuck!"

On and on it went. He didn't let me sleep. He didn't let me rest. It was rolling pleasure again and again. Until the sun started peeking through the blinds. Until all the hate in Hamilton's body was spent. Until we both were ready to face the day ahead.

20

HAMILTON

I woke up to Little Mama whining. I'd probably slept a total of two hours, and my dick felt like it was about to fall off from all the extra work it put in last night. Fucking hell. Vera was lying in bed, her hair fanned out around her and her creamy skin marked up with hickeys. I got dressed and brushed my teeth. "Come on, girl," I said before grabbing Little Mama's leash off the nightstand. She squirmed, annoyed with how off our routine we were. Me too, girl. Me too.

Outside, a man pushing a cleaning cart walked by as we made our way to a patch of grass. My phone started ringing, and I looked at the screen while Little Mama took the biggest steaming pile of shit I'd ever seen.

It was Jack, probably wondering why I hadn't shown up at work. I wasn't ready to talk to him. I didn't even know what I was going to say to him. No. I wasn't answering it. I didn't want to hear his excuses. I didn't want to listen to him pretend to give a fuck about me. A car blaring rap music slowly drove by, and I irresponsibly left the shit on the ground for someone else to step in before walking back to our room. It was time to face the music.

The minute I slid our key card into the lock and opened the door, I heard Vera's frantic voice. "Mom?" Vera said while sitting up. She clutched the hotel sheets to her body while staring off in the distance. "Mom? You have to speak up. I can't understand what you're saying."

My eyes thinned to slits, and I cocked my head to the side in question. "Joseph," Vera's voice cracked. Seeing my girl on the brink of passing out sobered me up from the stupor I was in.

I rubbed my eyes for a second before mouthing, "What's wrong?"

Vera ignored me and gasped. "No. No, don't hurt her. I'll be right there."

I grabbed the phone out of her hand and held it up to my ear. My girl looked to be in shock. "Who is this?" I asked.

"Oh hey, brother. I figured your little slut was with you. I was thinking, we should have a family reunion."

My blood chilled at his words. "What do you want?"

"Exactly that, Hamilton. A reunion. I was thinking about pie. I want a piece to eat in peace. Hell, I'd buy an entire bakery at this point."

"You sound fucking psychotic. What is going on?" I pressed on.

"Right, right. I guess I'm not feeling myself. I've got so many thoughts, you know? So much anger. Dad was angry, too. But not anymore. Lilah keeps fucking sobbing when I need her to mop up the blood. Oh my goodness, are you on your way yet? Stop and get me a pie—cherry pie."

I'd always known my brother was insane, but this took things to an entirely different level. What the fuck was wrong with him? "Joseph, what do you mean *blood*?"

"You told me to run, but I remembered something particularly important, Hamilton. I'm a Beauregard. I don't run. I bloody up the competition. Fuck, I'm hungry. Hurry up and get here, okay?"

Joseph hung up the phone.

Shit. Shit, shit, shit. My brother had completely lost his mind.

I took a moment to organize my thoughts and go over everything he'd said.

Dad was angry, too. But not anymore.

Lilah keeps fucking sobbing.

I need her to mop up the blood...

I need her to mop up the blood...

I need her to mop up the blood...

I need her to mop up the blood...

I need her to mop up the blood...

Vera was searching the floor for her clothes. She could barely stand up, her legs were so weak and shaky from the adrenaline. "We have to go. He has my mom. He told me to come over with you if I want her to live. What's happening, Hamilton?" She broke down, falling to her knees while sobbing uncontrollably. There was no way in hell I'd have her walk into this trap.

"I'm going to call the police," I said.

Vera gasped and clutched her chest. "He'll kill her, Hamilton. You can't."

"I'm not playing his game, Vera. What other option do we have, storm into the house and let him kill us too?"

She dragged her sharp nails down the sides of her face before letting out a harsh scream. "It's not a game, Hamilton! She could die!"

Fuck.

"Okay. I'll go. Call the police when—"

Vera stood up and grabbed my arm, digging her nimble fingers into my flesh with her glossy eyes wide with fear and looking up at me. "You're not going there alone, Hamilton."

"What choice do I have, Petal?"

A terrible, intrusive thought slammed into me. It was selfish and wrong. So dark that I didn't dare articulate it to Vera even though I knew deep in my gut that she was thinking it too.

So what if Joseph killed Lilah?

"I'm going to go with you. Call Saint. He has a gun, doesn't he?

I let out a huff. Surprisingly enough, my brother was probably better at being levelheaded in this situation. I turned around and picked up my cell off the nightstand as Vera continued to get dressed. After dialing Saint's number, I watched my girl try to pull herself together as it rang.

"Yo, what's up?"

"Joseph is at Jack's house. He's manic as fuck. Threatening Lilah. Not sure what's up with Jack, but there was a mention of blood. He's threatening to kill her if we don't show up."

"No. Don't negotiate with the insane person. God, I thought I'd have to fight to be the favorite brother, but Joseph makes my job incredibly easy, doesn't he?"

"Not the appropriate time for jokes, asshole."

"So call the police. I mean, if Joseph is going postal, then this is the evidence we need. They're more capable of handling a hostage situation than we are."

Fuck. Okay. It was a risk we'd have to take. Lilah dug her grave when she stubbornly refused to leave. My number one priority was Vera, and I wasn't going to risk her or myself in this situation. "Meet me at Jack's house," I told Saint.

Vera swallowed and stared up at me as if I had all the answers. "What are we going to do?" she asked. I needed to be strong for my girl and help her get through this. I hung up the phone.

"Come on. Saint is going to meet us there, and we'll try to get inside. Go get in the car, I'll be out in a minute. I'm going to set out some food for Little Mama and tell Jess to come here, okay? I promise I'll help you save your mother, Vera." She nodded, not even questioning me. I just hoped she'd forgive me if I was making the wrong choice. For the first time in my life, I wasn't going to be reckless. And it was all for her. She nodded and left the hotel room in a shocked daze.

I picked up my phone, sent a quick text to Jess, asking her to pick up Little Mama from the hotel, before dialing 911.

"911, what's your emergency?"

"Hello, I'd like to report a possible hostage situation."

———

I COULD HEAR THE SIRENS LONG BEFORE I PULLED MY car down the winding road leading to my childhood home. Vera started hyperventilating. I saw the worry in her expression. I felt the guilt as if it were my own. Who knows how long Joseph had been there fucking with Lilah? While we were...were...

"The cops are here," she wailed. "Who called

them? Do you think it was Jack? What if Joseph hurt Mom?" I didn't answer her; instead, I pressed on the gas pedal a little harder. "Do you think Jack is dead?" Vera whispered.

I hadn't even allowed myself the time to think about what that would mean. There was no love lost between my father and me, but there was so much unfinished business I didn't know where to begin. I craved closure. How was I supposed to navigate the truth of what he had planned for me if I never got the opportunity for justice?

Justice and revenge were two sides of the same coin. It was a currency my family thrived on, and now I was looking at the possibility of never claiming the debt owed to me.

Dozens of police cars lined the drive. Flashing blue and red lights assaulted my vision. Neighbors were marching up the road to see what was going on. It was only a matter of time before the paparazzi showed up. They tried directing my car away, but I put it in park and got outside.

"Sir, you can't come here." The officer held up his hands and nodded at the car. "Get back in your car and move." He was a shorter man with a buzzcut, a bored gaze, and a large nose.

"I'm Hamilton Beauregard. My brother, father, and sister-in-law are all in that house."

The police's face flashed into sympathy, and Vera stumbled out of the car toward us. She shivered as a gust of icy wind blasted her. Shit. I didn't even grab her a jacket. "Come with me," the officer replied.

We made our way to the front of the line of cars, where frantic officers were putting up a police line and yelling into radios. "I don't care if you have to drag Detective Burns out of his honeymoon bed with a condom still wrapped around his dick. We've got a hostage situation at the governor's house, and he's the most talented negotiator we have."

I cleared my throat. The officer yelling demands into this radio was tall, muscular, and had a missing front tooth. I noted a tattoo curling around his neck. I guess he wasn't your typical blue-collar cop. "Who is this? Who are you?" He nodded at Vera and me.

"I'm Hamilton Beauregard. I made the call after Joseph called me this morning." Vera gasped and looked at me as if I'd betrayed her. "I'm sorry, Petal. I had to make the decision that would keep us safe. I'm not giving in to Joseph's demands."

It felt unnatural to not let Joseph win. Vera looked wounded, but I'd grovel for the rest of my life if it meant keeping her safe. She looked at me before speaking. "We'll talk about this later. Is my mother in there? Is she okay?" Vera interrupted, her eyes filled with tears. I wrapped my arm around her and stared the officer down. Thankfully, she didn't push me away. I knew I'd made the right choice. Soon, she'd know it too.

"Tell me everything you know, Beauregard."

"Answer my girl's question, first," I snapped back.

The officer rolled his eyes and ran his hand over his bald head to wipe back some sweat. From where I was standing, I could see the house clearly. "I'm Officer Gideon. We had officers approach the house approximately thirteen minutes after receiving a call. Upon arriving, Joseph Beauregard opened the door and aimed a firearm at both officers, telling them to leave. One officer saw blood on the ground and covering Joseph's face, hands, and torso. The other saw a woman later identified as Lilah Beauregard crouched in a corner. Both retreated after the suspect made demands."

"What demands?" I asked.

He looked me up and down. "You said your name was Hamilton?"

I furrowed my brow. "Yes?"

The officer looked around before lowering his voice. "He demanded to speak with you."

Vera pressed the back of her hand to her mouth and whimpered. "So what are we going to do?" I asked. "What's your plan?"

Officer Gideon exhaled. "The plan is for you to tell me every goddamn thing you know. We won't make any moves until the negotiator is here. We don't know if Gov. Beauregard is dead. We don't know who all is on the premises. Right now, we wait."

"Let me through, asshole!" I heard Saint shout. I looked over my shoulder at my determined brother, suddenly feeling relieved that he was here. We'd started this revenge game together, and it looked like we'd end it together, too.

"Let him in!" I yelled to the officer blocking Saint from coming any closer.

"The weirdo wearing a pink bow tie and a neon shirt with the word *Penis* on the front is with you?" Officer Gideon deadpanned. Yeah, he was weird as hell, but we were family.

I let out a puff of air. "That weirdo has evidence that Gov. Jack Beauregard was plotting to murder me. He also found proof that Joseph Beauregard is laundering millions of dollars through Beauregard Industries."

Vera chewed on her nails. Saint smirked. Officer

Gideon looked like he wanted to be anywhere but here. I'm sure he was already counting up the mess of paperwork and press involved.

"Well, let him through," Gideon replied. "Someone bring me a pack of cigarettes!"

21

VERA

My mother was in that house. Despite the world of difference separating us lately, I instinctively knew in my gut that she was still alive. She had to be. We had so much left to fix.

"Vera? Are you there?" Anika asked.

The portable heater the state police set up wasn't nearly enough to thaw the chill in my muscles. I let out a sigh before responding. "We're still here. The negotiator has been trying to get Joseph on the phone for the last hour." In the six long hours since we'd arrived, the FBI had arrived, the press had started lining the street a half mile away, and some of the police officers had set up a tent that acted as a temporary headquarters. I told and retold my version of events to Officer Gideon and then later told the FBI agent who took over. I'd answered questions until my voice was hoarse. Thankfully, they let me take a break while Hamilton and Saint shared the laundering information they'd drummed up. I wasn't allowed to tell Anika much since it was an ongoing hostage situation, but hearing her voice settled me.

"I'm so sorry this is happening, Vera. Can I bring you anything? It sounds like your teeth are chattering, I can drive some warm clothes up to you."

I was already wearing a coat. It wasn't the chill in the air that had me chattering. It was the adrenaline. I felt wired and drained all at once. "I could just use some wisdom," I admitted.

Anika paused for a moment. "I don't think pretty words are what you need right now. I think you need to scream. There is nothing I can say that will make this situation easier to swallow. It's not the time for looking deep within yourself and seeking the answers to life through some philosophical lens. It's time to let the pain out, Vera. You don't have to be strong. You're allowed to be scared. You're allowed to cry and worry about your mom, okay? You're also allowed to be angry."

I looked to my left at Hamilton, who was pointing at something on a laptop. Most of all, I felt numb. I felt like I had somehow shut off my mind so I could navigate the crazy that was happening. "I have a lot to work through," I admitted. I was still angry with Hamilton for lying to me and calling the police, but admittedly, it was the right call. We weren't equipped to handle something like this. I just hated feeling out of control. "I just hate sitting here waiting."

"Let me know if I can bring you anything. I'm here for you, Vera."

"Thank you," I replied in a monotone voice. I was so withdrawn.

"Okay. Let me know if you need anything. I'm here for you, okay?" she repeated.

"Thanks, Anika."

I hung up the phone and stared at the front door of Jack's home, thinking back on the wedding we'd hosted here and all the things that had happened after that. There were men in full body armor standing around, but no one looked on alert. It was like they weren't taking it seriously, just waiting out the tantrum of a toddler.

"Are we just going to sit here all day?" I asked, my voice shrill and loud.

One of the agents looked at me, then continued to type on their computer. Hamilton excused himself and walked over to me. "Petal, if you want to leave, we can—"

"I'm not leaving!" I growled. "My mom might be a shitty mother, and I might no longer feel obligated to bend and snap to her will, but I don't want her to die! What if I never get the chance to fix my relationship with her? What if we never speak again?" My chest tightened, and Hamilton hugged me fiercely.

"The FBI is handling this. It's all going to be okay, Petal."

"Is it?" I asked in a high-pitched voice. "Is it going to be okay? Or is our life going to be the constant war of bullshit power plays orchestrated by your family?"

"I get that you're upset right now, but—"

"Stop talking and just hold me, please," I cracked. Hamilton didn't hesitate for a second, his hold on me tightened, and I let his strength wash over me.

"It's going to be okay," he said in a soothing tone once more.

Someone shouted, and it sent a ripple of alertness through everyone. Hamilton let go of me, and I turned to look at the source of the commotion. "Someone is at the front door!" I immediately broke away from Hamilton and moved to see what was going on behind the safety of a line of armored cars. Hamilton trailed closely behind me, his fingers holding onto my shirt, as if he were afraid I'd run toward the house.

There stood Joseph. He had one hand on a gun, one arm wrapped around my mother. Both of them were covered in blood.

I swallowed the vomit threatening to travel up my throat and cried. "Oh, God!"

"Get her out of here!" one of the agents hissed. Hamilton tried to move me back, but I planted my feet on the ground, determined to see what was happening.

"Bring me Hamilton and Vera!" Joseph cried out. "I want a fucking family reunion, or the bitch dies!" Joseph pulled my mother in front of him, treating her like a human shield. It was the most horrific thing I'd ever seen.

Time stopped. Horror made me freeze on the spot. Joseph was this feral entity, challenging the world with his crazed eyes and curled lip.

A man with slicked back hair and a bulletproof vest carefully walked forward with his hands up. I recognized him as the negotiator. "Joseph? Hi, my name is—"

Joseph didn't even let him introduce himself. Instead, he shot a bullet in the air with a loud war cry. Some of the officers ducked. I stood in a panic-stricken freeze. "Shit," Hamilton cursed before Joseph resumed pressing the barrel of his gun back against my mother's temple.

"I can't get a clear shot," someone said over the radio.

Joseph screamed. "I told you my demands. Bring me Vera and Hamilton. FUCKING NOW. I'm in control. I have all the power. You can't bring me down. I'm fucking untouchable!" His roars sounded insane.

"What happened to Jack, Joseph? Is he inside?" the negotiator asked through a bullhorn. He sounded nasally but calm.

"He's DEAD!" Joseph laughed. "Dead!"

A frantic murmur broke out in the crowd around me. Mom started sobbing loudly, which seemed to piss off Joseph. Hamilton dropped his mouth open in disbelief. I grabbed his hand and squeezed, providing silent comfort.

Mom's cries grew even louder, apparently pissing off Joseph even more. "Shut the fuck up, you stupid slut!" She pressed her hands over her face and silently cried, obeying him despite the obvious distress she was under.

"Joseph. We can negotiate. You don't have to be charged with two murders today," the negotiator called out.

"Fuck you. Where is my brother? I know he's out there. I can sense his weakness."

"I'm right here, you motherfucker," Hamilton yelled out. I spun to stare at him.

"What are you doing?" I hissed.

"Stand down," another agent demanded.

Hamilton ignored the furious looks he was getting. "If Joseph wants to talk to me, then I'll fucking talk to him," he said in a low voice before shouting at Joseph. "Come meet me like a man! Stop hiding behind your wife."

The negotiator cursed but quickly waved Hamilton forward. Hamilton accepted the bulletproof vest that one of the agents held out to him and took a few steps toward the negotiator. "Don't rile him up," the negotiator instructed. I couldn't help but think that Hamilton was the wrong man for the job if we were trying to keep Joseph calm. Their entire relationship was about riling each other up.

"You don't know what it means to be a man!" he roared. "You don't know what it's like to have blood on your hands. To see the light in their eyes dim."

I took a tentative step toward the house—toward Joseph. One of the agents reached out to stop me, but Joseph shot another bullet into the air. "No one stop Vera and Hamilton from coming, or I'll shoot her. I'll kill her right now, and I don't care if I go with her. Till death do us part, right, honey?"

My mother whimpered.

"It's too late, Joseph," Hamilton called out. He moved to stand beside me at the very edge of the police line, still protected by the line of cars, but with a clear view of the insanity happening in front of us. We clasped our hands together, determined to face this together. I tried to sense if Hamilton was shocked or disturbed by the news of his father's death, but he kept his face passive and emotionless. I couldn't tell if he was just being strong for the moment or for his own sanity. "You have no power here."

Joseph's lip curled, and he started heaving. "You're wrong."

"Look around, Joseph!" Hamilton yelled. The negotiator casually observed the back and forth, processing it. Another officer whispered at our backs.

"Keep him talking."

I swallowed. "Mom, are you okay?" I called out.

She finally removed her hands from her face and scanned the crowd. When her eyes landed on me, she breathed a sigh of relief. "I'm okay, baby."

"Shut the fuck up!" Joseph yelled before kicking the back of her heel. She almost fell forward, but the arm he had wrapped around her slender body kept her up. "I'll fuck your worthless cunt in front of all these people with a gun to your head, whore. I will. And I won't think twice about it."

I felt sick to my stomach, but the only thing keeping me calm was the fact that I had no other choice.

"Why did you kill Jack?" Hamilton asked.

"IT'S ALL YOUR FAULT! I've done everything he ever asked," Joseph replied, his voice softer. I almost didn't quite hear him. "I was the perfect son.

The perfect employee. I did it all. And he wanted to betray me like this? Fuck that."

"Why not let him rot in jail?" Hamilton asked.

"It wasn't enough. I wanted him to pay. I thought you'd be happy, Hamilton. I thought you'd like knowing I took out dear old dad!" The tension in the air was so thick it couldn't even be cut with a knife.

"You should have run, Joseph," Hamilton said.

"And you should have never been born!" Joseph screamed back. "MOM GAVE YOU EVERYTHING! EVERYTHING WAS LEFT TO YOU. How could she love a fucking bastard?!"

I noticed movement from behind, a man wearing all black was ascending on Joseph. The glock in his hand looked threatening. I didn't understand how they would take him down without hurting my mother. Joseph had his finger on the trigger. One wrong move and...

"Fuck you. Fuck all of you. You have no idea what it takes to be a Beauregard! It's power like you wouldn't believe!" The man got closer to Joseph, and I had to force myself not to flinch or stare too hard.

Hamilton took a deep breath and pulled me closer. "I'm a god!" Joseph yelled. "And you are nothing."

The man moved swiftly and placed the gun to

Joseph's temple. Not even a second passed before the man pulled the trigger. Mom screamed. I cried out. Blood and brain covered my mother's face. Soaked the front porch. Filled my vision. Joseph's prone, lifeless body collapsed to the ground, taking my mother with him. They both fell in a puddle of his gore. Mom squirmed and cried out, trying to get away from his death grip. Federal agents ran toward her. So much blood.

Flesh.

Hair.

A fractured skull dripping with crimson death.

Hamilton stepped in front of me, his own eyes wide from the trauma of what we just witnessed. I couldn't believe it. That was—

"Look at me, Petal. Don't look at them. Look at me." I started to breathe heavily. Somewhere in the distance, men were shouting and my mother was screaming so loudly that her voice cut through her rough vocal cords. More and more. I closed my eyes, and the only thing I saw was Joseph's head exploding again and again and again.

"Open your eyes, Petal. Look at me. It's all going to be okay."

I obeyed Hamilton, shocked that he could even form sentences after what just happened. Part of me wanted to run to my mother, but the other part of me was still too stunned. My toes, shins, thighs, stomach, arms, fingers, chest, neck, cheeks, each inch of my body turned cold. "You're in shock, Vera. I need you to move. Can I get some help here?"

"Mom?" I croaked before pushing at his chest. Hamilton didn't budge, but I needed to see that she was okay. My throat dried. My vision blurred. "Mom!"

"Baby!" she cried out. One beat of my heart. Two beats. I inhaled, exhaled. Blinking twice, I grabbed hold of a portion of my sanity and pushed past Hamilton to check on my mother. She was wrapped in the arms of Officer Gideon and trying to walk toward me, but her legs kept failing. I pushed through the crowd toward her, crying at the sight of blood coating her skin.

We collided painfully. I forced myself not to vomit when she hugged me tight. I held my breath as she sobbed against me. I looked up at the sky when she started repeating the same thing over and over and over:

He's dead.

He's dead.

He's dead.

22

VERA

*M*om looked so frail in the hospital bed. She was staying the night out of an abundance of caution. She had bruises along her jaw and neck, but it was her mind that needed the most healing. The chair I was sitting on wasn't comfortable, but I couldn't sleep. Every time I closed my eyes, I saw him. I saw the death. I saw the blood. I heard her screams.

A nurse walked in, clipboard in hand. She

quietly slid back the curtain and whispered to me. "Just want to check her vitals really quick, is that okay?"

I rubbed my nose and nodded. "Sure."

With caring eyes, the woman peered at me. I didn't like the pity in her gaze. Hamilton was out getting coffee and some fresh air. I'd been leaning on him for support, but we both needed time to individually process everything that had happened, too.

"The crowd outside is insane. Police had to escort me in for my shift today, can you imagine? It's so impolite. Don't they have any respect?" she asked while checking the machines hooked up to my mother and her IV.

I didn't even want to think about what was going on outside or what rumors were circulating. My mother was living with Jack when her ex-husband murdered him.

Yes, murdered.

Fifteen bullets. Joseph emptied fifteen bullets in his father. I hadn't seen Jack's body, but I couldn't help but visualize Swiss cheese. His body was full of holes, battered and bloody.

"Do you need a blanket, honey?" the nurse asked. I shook my head, and she frowned at me. I didn't want her sympathy. I wanted her silence. I wanted a bit of peace. "This whole situation is just so insane. If you'd like, I can have the hospital send a counselor to your room? It's been a traumatic day for both of you."

"I don't want to talk about how I saw a man shot in the head today. I just want to sleep," I snapped back with a tight smile. "Please." I added the pleasantry as an afterthought.

The slim, older nurse nodded. "I know it's hard to see the positive in things right now. But at least the baby survived."

I frowned. "What baby?"

The nurse furrowed her brow and checked her chart. "It says here your mom is six weeks pregnant. The sonographer found a heartbeat earlier while you were talking to the police."

All the moisture in my mouth disappeared. Oh my God. "Baby? My mother is pregnant?"

The nurse nodded. "I thought you knew."

"Six weeks?" I asked, my hand pressed to my chest. I tried to mentally do the math. Did that mean Jack was the father? Or was it Joseph?

Mom moaned and shifted on the mattress. I stood up. "It's the little blessings, you know?" the nurse said, as if she were proud of herself for spewing wisdom, optimism, and hope. Didn't she know? A baby was the last thing my mother needed. "I'll let you rest. Press the call button if you need anything, dear."

Once the nurse was gone, I took a moment to hover over my mother. I stared at the bruise on her jaw, the cut on her lip, the tangles in her matted hair. She looked so naïve and innocent at that moment. Staring at her made rage travel up my throat.

No. That wasn't rage, it was vomit.

I placed my hand over my mouth and grabbed a nearby trashcan before voiding the entire contents of my stomach into it. I'd barely eaten in the last forty-eight hours. It was nothing but dry heaving and acid rolling around my mouth.

"Baby?" Mom murmured. "You okay?"

I straightened my spine and wiped my mouth with the back of my hand. "Who is the daddy, Mom?"

Her eyes widened. "Vera...I-I'm tired can we please discuss this later? It's been such an awful day." Tears welled up in her eyes, and I suddenly realized that Lilah Garner wasn't worth the confrontation. I wasn't going to shame her for getting pregnant or for getting in this situation at all. "Can you please just hold my hand. I need support now more than ever, Vera. We will be in this together. Maybe get an apartment and—"

"I'm glad you're safe, Mom," I murmured before standing up and moving to grab my purse.

"Are you going to get food? I'm really hungry…"

"I'm going home. With Hamilton."

She got a puzzled look on her face. "Home? But I won't get discharged until tomorrow. I had a very traumatic day, Vera. You can't seriously think you'll just leave me here. The love of my life just died!" Her choice of words baffled me. She needed help.

It was on the tip of my tongue to ask her who she was talking about. Two men died today. Did she mourn Jack, her false hero? Or Joseph, the man who broke her but brought her into this life of luxury?

There was so much love in my heart for Lilah. Today was a hard slap to the face that this life was temporary, and I didn't want to spend the rest of my days resenting her or hating her for who she was. It took a lot of work to feel a constant thread of resentment. I was done with that.

"I love you, Mom," I whispered before sitting on the edge of the bed. She smiled at me, like my devotion was something cute she could put in her pocket and think fondly of. "I'm glad you're okay. The doctors said you could be discharged tomorrow.

Do you know where you're going to stay?" I asked softly.

"Well, with you, of course. I'm a widow. I can't stay in that house where...where..." Her voice trailed off, and she stared over my head with glassy eyes. It was as if she was no longer in this hospital room, she was reliving what happened at Jack's house. "We were in bed," she whispered. "Jack and I. Joseph just showed up. He laughed when he saw me, though. Like he didn't even care..."

I patiently listened to her. She licked her lips, and the heart monitor strapped to her chest started going faster. "Joseph dragged Jack downstairs to the living room. I followed after them. It was so fast, you know. He pissed on Jack first. Unzipped his pants and just..."

"Mom," I began softly. "You went through a lot. I think you need to talk to someone. About this. About Joseph hurting you. About me, even." I reached out and pushed her sweaty hair behind her ear. She was like a child, staring up at me, her mouth agape, her eyes filled with unshed tears.

"I'm talking to you, though, baby."

I let out a huff of air. "Do you remember that apartment we had back in Atlanta, Mom?" I asked. "I loved that place. We had the wall where you marked how tall I was getting. We'd have sleepovers in the tiny living room and watch TV until the sun came up. It was such a special place, don't you think? And then the roof caved in one day."

Mom rolled her eyes. "That was a nightmare. Everything was ruined. Fire marshal made us all evacuate because it wasn't livable anymore. We had nowhere to go."

I nodded. It was part of the reason we ended up moving to Connecticut. "You've always been my home, Mom. You let me live, and breathe, and grow in a safe space, and I will forever be thankful for that." Mom reached out and squeezed my hand. I gave her a tight grin. "But your home isn't livable anymore. You have so much work to do. Walls to rebuild. A foundation that's cracked. There's a lot of damage, but I think you are more than capable of working from the ground up and creating something so much better than before. And I hope you don't do it for me or for the men you date or the life you think you want. Not even for the baby growing inside of you right now. I need you to build yourself up for you. I found a new home, and it's with Hamilton."

Mom's face twisted up in pain. The cut on her lip

cracked, and a few drops of blood spilled. She wiped at them with her hand. "Baby..."

I stood up. "You have my number. I love you so much. I'm here for you. I just need a little time, and you have a home to rebuild."

She cradled her head in her hands and sobbed as I walked out of the room. I couldn't help but feel hopeful about our relationship. My mom taught me a lot of things, but the most important lesson was how to love someone while still loving myself.

Today, Jack and Joseph Beauregard were quietly buried side by side at Groves Creek Cemetery. Reporters said it was a quiet affair, not even the housekeeper attended.

I certainly didn't.

I wore an all-black suit and despite not shedding a single tear for either one of them, my eyes were red. "Reservation for Hamilton Beauregard," I said to the hostess. Vera grabbed my arm and squeezed. I could sense the slight apprehension in her. The last time we were at this restaurant, we ended up confronting Jack.

There was nothing left living on this earth that would stop me from sitting at my mother's favorite restaurant and enjoying her memory. "Right this way, Mr. Beauregard," the hostess said. I wrapped my arm around Vera, who snuggled into my side. She spent the entire day watching me, waiting for me to break. She'd say things that were so perfectly *Vera*.

"It's okay to mourn them, Hamilton."

"No one will judge you if you want to go to the funeral. Or if you want to stay home. I'm here, whatever you want to do. We don't always choose our family, but they're ours."

"I love you, Hamilton. I'm here for you."

I loved my girl. I loved her so much that I kept the burning truth buried deep in my chest. Honestly, I didn't care that Jack and Joseph were dead. I loved knowing that right now they were no longer a threat to society, they were no longer a threat to Vera.

They couldn't hurt anyone anymore. They couldn't lie anymore.

"I'll have sparkling water," Vera told the waitress.

"Bring me some gin! I'm celebrating tonight!" Jess said while marching up to us. I got up to give her a hug beside our table. She was wearing a rose-colored tuxedo and heels. Beside her, Infinity was in a long green dress with tears all over it. I grinned at my best friend, the person who had always been a constant in my life. "Are we doing shots? I think the occasion calls for it." Leave it to Jess to say exactly how I was feeling.

"Maybe later," I whispered in her ear before returning to my seat.

Vera smiled at the door and took a deep breath. I followed her gaze and forced my face into a pleasant expression at the sight of Lilah and Vera's old professor, Anika. Surprisingly, the two of them had been bonding. Lilah was still a piece of shit in my mind, but she'd mellowed out some. Vera connected the two of them when Lilah said she wanted help but didn't want to speak to a therapist. Apparently, they were meeting for lunch daily. It made my girl happy, so I was willing to play nice. As long as Lilah worked on herself and didn't upset Vera, I was fine with their albeit distant, but still meaningful, relationship.

"Hey, baby. You look nice," Lilah said before nervously tucking her hair behind her ear.

"You look good, too, Mom," Vera replied. "How are you feeling?"

"Good. A little nauseous..."

Yeah. That was fucking insane. Vera and I were no longer related, but in a few months, we would share a half sibling. I had to force myself not to think about it, or it made me uncomfortable.

"Hey, Hamilton. Thank you for, uh, inviting me."

I nodded at Lilah. The black dress she wore was simple and long. She didn't have a ridiculous amount of makeup on, and her hair was curled down her back. She also didn't have the usual black circles under her eyes. Despite being uncharacteristically timid, she seemed almost...normal.

Weirder things had happened, I suppose.

"How was your first week of class?" Anika asked Vera while holding her hands. I noticed Lilah watch Anika and Vera with jealousy and longing. I could understand it. Anika checked on Vera daily and helped her prepare for her first semester at her new university. She had somehow become a motherly figure in Vera's life, filling a role Lilah was incapable of filling.

"It was really good. I like my professors. The commute is long but worth it. Did I tell you about my new ethics professor?" The three of them sat down at the table, Anika and Vera excitedly chatting while Lilah interjected occasionally.

Standing alone and waiting, I felt my nerves start to kick in. I swallowed my emotions and adjusted my tie. I'd never felt so unsteady. This felt like a defining moment. I'd been both dreading and anticipating it all day. The door to the restaurant opened, and Saint walked in, wearing a sequined jacket and purple pants. His hair was slicked to the side, and he had an excited look on his face.

I was happy to see my brother. This entire experience had bonded us in a way. But it wasn't he who had me squirming where I stood, it was the beautiful woman on his arm that made my breath catch.

She had brown hair like mine, a long neck, a nervous smile that still somehow managed to brighten the room. She wore a long navy dress, nude heels, and a silver clutch. She looked around the room with trepidation, but eventually her eyes landed on me.

Saint guided her toward me, each step felt like it took a lifetime. Sweat dripped down the side of my face. What if she didn't like me? What if she wasn't what I expected? What if she was just another person who hurt me? What if one day she left just like Mom did?

Vera settled at my side and swiftly grabbed my hand. "I'm so proud of you, Hamilton," she whispered in that silent, reassuring way of hers. I leaned over to kiss the top of her head, just as Saint arrived in front of me with our mother.

"I like the suit," I told Saint before looking at *her* once more. Up close, I could see so much of myself in her features. The strong nose. Smirking lips. Playful determination in her gaze.

"Hamilton," she breathed. "It's really nice to finally meet you."

"Hey," I replied awkwardly.

"Can I hug you please? I've just...I've always wanted to hu—"

I cut her words off by closing the distance between us and wrapping my arms around her. She smelled like a fresh garden, and her slender shoulders trembled as she quietly cried. When we pulled away, she wiped at her eyes. "There's just so much to talk about. I've missed so much..."

This reunion was beautiful, but still bittersweet. "We have all the time in the world."

Gabby nodded and another happy tear fell from her eyes. "Thank you for meeting me. I know I'm not

Nikki. But I really hope you'll give me the chance to love you, Hamilton." She stared at me for a moment longer, as if cataloguing my features before digging in her purse. "I wanted to give you this."

She pulled out a long envelope and handed it to me. "Four months ago, I started cleaning out my house, and I found this letter. I had never opened it. I'm not sure how it got mixed up in my things. I want you to read it, when you're ready. But more importantly, it led me to a safety deposit box at United Trust downtown where I found your mother's will, Hamilton."

Shock hit me full force. Mom sent her will to Gabby? That made no sense. "She sent it to you?" I asked in disbelief before taking the envelope from her hands.

"Somehow the letter got mixed up in a box of junk. I never saw it, never opened it. Things were really bad for me around that time with the divorce and losing my job. If I had known..."

"Are you the person that sent this to Jack?" I asked while staring down at the paper. Saint averted his eyes. "Did you know about this?" I asked my brother.

"I didn't tell a soul, Hamilton," Gabby interrupted. "Saint didn't know. I already hate that he constantly puts himself in danger. I didn't want him to have anything to do with this. I know what Jack is capable of. He ruined my life."

"Who sent the will to Jack then?" I asked.

"I pulled every penny I had together and went to a lawyer to check the legality of this will. I wanted the law on my side so I could bring this public and still protect you and Saint. But I think the lawyer saw an opportunity to blackmail Jack. He stopped taking my calls. He had his secretary cancel my appointments. It wasn't until the news broke out that I realized what had happened."

I blinked twice. "I can't believe she sent it to you."

"Hamilton, I wanted to start our relationship with no secrets. I truly hope you can forgive me for not coming to you with this. My only goal was to protect the two of you."

I held up my hand. "Thank you for telling me. I'm just... My mom wrote this letter?" I asked once more. It didn't matter how many times she said it, I still couldn't make sense of it. I didn't care about the money or the will or how Jack responded to that. I didn't care about anything.

"Yes, honey. Your mom wrote that letter to me."

I slowly opened the envelope, and Vera, God

fucking love her, guided them to the table so I could read it in peace.

DEAR GABBY,

I'm so terribly sorry.

You must hate me, Gabby. How is it possible that I got to raise your son while you got nothing? Jack told me you wanted this, but I know that now to be untrue. My husband isn't afraid to hurt people to maintain the status quo.

And I can't bring myself to care if you miss Hamilton. He's mine—at least for now—in all the ways that count. I might not be good enough, but I love him. He has the most compassionate heart. His capacity to love and do good is so, so great. I know the only good my son has comes from you. Jack and I simply aren't capable of it.

Thank you for letting me love your son. I'm sure it was a heavy sacrifice to have your heart living and breathing outside of your chest, coddled and cared for by someone else. Thank you for giving me the greatest love of my life. Maybe it's selfish of me to have favorites. I love both my children, but I feel my love for Hamilton just a little bit deeper.

I'm writing you this letter because I won't be on this earth much longer. You see, I'm not well, Gabby. Jack keeps grinding me down, hoping to mold the perfect wife to sit upon his shelf. He hurts me, Gabby. Did he ever hurt you? It's wrong and debilitating. The drugs help a little, but I find myself wanting to take handfuls of them. I can sit here and count up all the reasons why I should try again, fight again. But the list doesn't feel nearly as important as the impending doom I sense. It's a tragic cliché to write a suicide letter to a virtual stranger, but I feel like I know you. I've seen your soul through the eyes of our son. And I need you to help protect him from Jack. Enclosed are details about a safety deposit box. Please go to it and follow the instructions upon my death.

There is so much I want to teach Hamilton, but the most important message is something you can help me with. Teach him about love, Gabby—the kind of love that is limitless. Teach him about family, too. I'm afraid Jack, Joseph and I have failed him in that department. I hope my son never feels the loneliness I feel. I hope he never feels empty.

Thank you. For everything.

Yours,

Nikki

THE PAPER WAS STAINED WITH MY TEARS BY THE TIME I read the last line. I looked up to stare at the table full of people that loved me and I loved back. I wiped my nose and folded the paper while looking up at the ceiling of Mom's favorite restaurant before moving toward Vera. She quietly stood up and took my hand. In her eyes, I saw love. "You okay?" she asked softly.

I leaned forward to kiss her on the forehead. I didn't want to dwell on the letter or the lack of closure I still felt. My mother probably had high hopes that Gabby would step up and be the mother she was too broken to be. She wanted me to learn about love and family.

But it wasn't my birth mother that taught me just how limitless and healing love could be. It was the beautiful, kind, and caring girl standing in front of me. Vera softly blinked and waited patiently for me to speak.

"I love you," I whispered.

"I love you too," she replied.

Jess whistled before stopping the heavy moment with a loud smack of her palms hitting together. "I thought we were celebrating the Wicked Witch of the East's death?"

Vera bit the inside of her cheek, likely trying to be polite for my sake.

I stared at her for a minute longer before guiding

her back to her seat. "I think I'm going to order the spaghetti. Mom loved spaghetti," I began. Everyone seemed to breathe a sigh of relief. Long gone was the self-destructive asshole. I could handle remembering her. I could compartmentalize the good while still grieving the pain she felt she couldn't escape.

Normal chatter picked up.

"I'm just going to deep throat some breadsticks," Saint interjected.

Lilah laughed so hard that she nearly choked on her own spit.

"Have I mentioned that I like your brother, Hamilton? I really like him..." Jess added.

And on and on it went. The banter and familiarity. I looked around the table and saw something that made my heart swell.

Family.

I had family.

EPILOGUE

Vera

Four Years Later

"*I*'m not fucking you in this hallway, Hamilton," I rasped out. My boyfriend was feeling particularly horny today. He ran his hands up and down my body, pressing me against the wall and not giving a single fuck that people were walking by. I looked up at him with a smirk on my face.

"Vera, this graduation gown is better than any lingerie I've ever seen. Please tell me you're wearing nothing underneath," he teased before pressing his lips to the side of my neck. "Can I fuck you on top of your diploma? The bastard stole a majority of my girl's attention the last four years, so it seems only fair I get the last laugh."

"You're impossible," I replied before shoving at his chest. Hamilton looked sexy, and if we weren't running late, I might have taken him up on his offer. But we had places to be. People to see. Graduations to celebrate. "Anika would kill us if we showed up late to the party. And you know she's been on edge trying to potty train Benjamin."

"Did you hear what he did?" Hamilton asked before chuckling.

"Oh no. What now?" Our baby brother was a handful and a half, but oh so very loved.

"He found a pair of scissors and cut his hair. Lilah had to come over and put her new cosmetology license to good use and fix it. Guess her new hobby is coming in handy."

I burst out laughing. "You're kidding."

"He's pretty proud of himself, the little goblin."

I shook my head and grinned, in awe of how perfect my life had become. I lived with my wonderful boyfriend surrounded by our unconventional family. My mom finally had her life together, or at least as together as possible for someone like her. She was still unapologetically self-centered. When Anika mentioned that she wanted to have a baby of her own, they came to the surprising open adoption arrangement. I'd be lying if I said I wasn't worried that Mom would try to extort money out of the Beauregard fortune because of the pregnancy. But it turned out, she wanted freedom more than she wanted to start over as a mother. Hamilton set up an iron-clad trust fund for Benjamin, but gave Mom Jack's house to do whatever she wanted with it.

Hamilton and I never openly discussed it, but the gift was kind of our unspoken bribe to keep Mom from trying anything. We cared about our brother and wanted him to have a better life than what we had. The home sold for twenty-seven million dollars. Mom was happy, and my baby brother was being raised by the woman who'd kind of adopted me, too.

Hamilton stared at my lips, longing in his gaze. "We should get going," I whispered.

"We should." He leaned in closer, brushing his nose against mine. I started breathing heavily. Fucking Hamilton. "Oh Vera, if these people weren't here, you'd be on your knees with my cock in your mouth."

My heart rate spiked, and I looked around the hallway at the other students excitedly chatting with their families. Jess, Mom, Anika, Saint, and Infinity had already left to finish setting up for my party. "Oh really?" I asked before biting my lip. Hamilton loved it when I bit my lip.

"Come on, my perfect little tease," Hamilton whispered before wrapping his hand around my wrist and pulling me down the hall, outside, and to his car. He looked around the crowded parking lot before shoving me into the back seat and following after me. The second the door shut, I started frantically removing my gown and the dress underneath. Hamilton unbuttoned his pants.

"So tell me," he breathed while shoving our clothes away and pulling me onto his lap. "What's the next step?"

I lifted up slightly, bumping my head on the roof of his car. "I was thinking—" My words were cut off with a brash kiss from Hamilton. I gasped when he pulled away, and took a lingering moment to sink down on his cock. We both groaned at the contact. "Of borrowing a couple million dollars from my ridiculously rich boyfriend and starting a nonprofit."

"Oh?" he replied through clenched teeth. I bounced up and down while tossing my head back. It was cramped. It was raw. It was oh-so-perfect. Even after all this time, the passion between us was explosive. "And what kind of nonprofit do you want to start?"

I stopped fucking him for a moment. "A support network for teen moms," I whispered.

Hamilton stroked my hair and smiled at me. "I love your heart, Vera Garner."

I knew I should probably say something sentimental, but we had our entire lives for that. "And I love your cock, Hamilton Beauregard," I teased before resuming the beautiful work of riding him so hard that the car shook in the parking lot.

A NOTE FROM THE AUTHOR

Thank you so much for reading. I hope you enjoyed the conclusion to the Twisted Legacy Duet.

Subscribe to my newsletter and check out more of my books: **www.authorcoraleejune.com**

If you are a blogger or bookstagramer that would like to be the first to know about my upcoming releases, sign up for my masterlist: **https://bit.ly/2KuJmcD**

Grab a free book: **https://linktr.ee/CoraLeeFreebiesandGiveaways**

ACKNOWLEDGMENTS

This book would not have been possible without the support and love of Christina Santos, as well as Christine Estevez .

I would like to especially thank Katie Friend, Meggan Reed, HarleyQuinn Zaler, Savannah Richey, Lauren Campbell and Claire Jones for beta reading.

I would like to especially thank Kelsey Clayton for helping me get through a laundry list of self-doubt. Thank you for helping me work through the plot and for reassuring me during the process of completely rewriting this book.

I would also like to thank Desiree Hayman for her time and knowledge. Your support during the research process for this book was incredibly helpful.

I am grateful to all of those with whom we have had the pleasure to work with during this book. I'd like to especially recognize my editor, Helayna Trask. She always takes the time to dive into the worlds we create and make sure they are perfect for you all. I would also like to thank all the dedicated members of The Zone and Cora's Crew. And finally, thank you again to HarleyQuinn Zaler for this drool-worthy cover.

ABOUT THE AUTHOR

CoraLee June is an international bestselling romance writer who enjoys engaging projects and developing real, raw, and relatable characters. She is an English major from Texas State University and has had an intense interest in literature since her youth. She currently resides with her husband and two daughters in Dallas, Texas, where she enjoys long walks through the ice cream aisle at her local grocery store.

Stalk Me:

Facebook:
https://www.facebook.com/AuthorCoraleeJune/
Instagram:
instagram.com/authorcoraleejune
BookBub:
https://www.bookbub.com/profile/coralee-june
Newsletter:
www.authorcoraleejune.com

Printed in Great Britain
by Amazon